Seated Woman

Guillaume Apollinaire

Seated Woman

A Chronicle of France and America

*translated with a memoir
and other material by*
Timothy Mathews

Shearsman Books

First published in the United Kingdom in 2023 by
Shearsman Books Ltd
PO Box 4239
Swindon
SN3 9FN

Shearsman Books Ltd Registered Office
30–31 St. James Place, Mangotsfield, Bristol BS16 9JB
(this address not for correspondence)

www.shearsman.com

ISBN 978-1-84861-838-1

The text of Guillaume Apollinaire, *La Femme assise*, Éditions de la Nouvelle
Revue Française, Paris, 1920, translated here is the one established by
Michel Décaudin and published in Guillaume Apollinaire, *Œuvres en prose*,
Éditions Gallimard (Bibliothèque de la Pléiade), volume 1, Paris, 1977.

Contents

Acknowledgements

My greatest thanks go to Guillaume Apollinaire himself, for the unending source that he's been to me of wisdom, wit, generosity, and realism; and for the invention, but also the dedication needed to keep all those elements going at once in his life and art. I would also like to thank a few people for the ways they've continually reminded me of the interactions of translation, critical thought, affective engagement, and writing. Taken together, friendship, partnership, and translation seem especially well suited to the task of communicating across innumerable borders, and whether in conversation, in their practices, or the kindness and meticulousness they've shown in reading versions of these texts, Jane Fenoulhet, Raymond Geuss, Elaine Green, Sarah Kay, and Rod Mengham have been constant presences along the journey of this book.

I offer my special thanks to Henrietta Simson for her work in securing permissions, and her creativity in helping to bring to life the way I've tried to use the images; and to Tony Frazer for his inspiration, and his confidence in this book.

An earlier version of 'Invention and Disaster: *Le Poète assassiné*' was published in a special issue of *Thinking Verse*, volume 4, issue 2, 2014, *À la Recherche: Essays in Honour of Clive Scott.*

Elements in sections I and XII of *The Story Re-told: Memoir of a translation* featured in 'Provoked by Translation', published in a special issue of *Textual Cultures*, 15.1, 2022, *Creative Critical Provocations*, edited by Mathelinda Nabugodi and Christopher Ohge.

Chapter One

Originally from Maisons-Lafitte, Elvira Swig has a decided taste for horses, for horse-riding as well, and she makes remarkable paintings of them.

Even though she can't go riding now she often thinks of it, and when life is full of trouble she imagines herself at the gallop, and finds comfort in that.

She has seen some wondrous horses in the famous stables of her native town, but the ones she remembers with the greatest pleasure are the three horses harnessed to the troika of her lover, the Grand Duke André Petrovitch.

As white as snow, they were the most beautiful horses in the whole of Russia. They were valued at a million each. Their tails floated above the ground, they went like the wind, and the coachman holding the reins was as fat as you like.

From her earliest childhood Elvira had an unchained mind and a remarkable memory. She had never been a believer, but had always been superstitious. Her dreams forever turned to love, and as a girl she dreamed of pins, pikes and barriers, which is significant according to the findings of certain experts.

Her first lover was a doctor, a married man who was both very kind and very debauched. He took her when she was fifteen. He was thirty-six. She was unwell and he had come to minister to her needs. He was a thin man, of the kind who know all the refinements of love and corrupt the minds of women, but women would never fall in love with him. Their liaison began with a scandal, the cat came out of the bag when Elvira's mother discovered the secret. The suborner was prosecuted, and only got away with it because Elvira swore in her statement that she wasn't a virgin at the time. He was acquitted and remained enthusiastically grateful.

So there was Elvira given over to the depraved education of George the doctor and his taste for women, and he planted in her mind everything there is to know about vice.

In the winter of 1913 he took her to Monte-Carlo, and left her there on her own when he suddenly needed to go back to Paris. Replanov noticed her in the Casino: he was the foremost lawyer of Petrograd, then called St Petersburg, and he advised her to come to Russia with him.

"You'll be happy there," he would say. "You'll be like a daughter to me, my own daughter died and you look just like her. Do come, you'll not want for anything. You'll be like a queen. I'll treat you like my own daughter." And then respectfully but passionately he would kiss the tips of her fingers.

Replanov was the first to leave and as George was taking such a time to return, Elvira made up her mind to set out for Russia. She went to buy her ticket from Wagons-Lits, but she looked so young and in fact was so young that as a precondition she had to get the consent of her father. Old man Replanov had written him a monument to hypocrisy, because no sooner had Elvira set foot in Petrograd than he sold her to a vice club of which he was a member, and she became the mistress of the Grand Duke André Petrovitch. She spent seven months in Russia, and one day she spoke to me in the following way of her time amongst the Muscovites:

"My lover the Grand Duke was twenty-six years old. He was very handsome. I've never seen such a handsome man nor such a brutal one. He liked women and boys. He was more corrupt than George because cruelty would overcome every one of his scruples, and his arrogance made him practically delirious. The women, mostly French, who were the mistresses of the other members of the club were neither young nor attractive. As far as I could tell they were all business women who indulged anything that struck the imagination of their lovers, which was depraved in the extreme. The prettiest was a Russian. She was also the most lascivious and her tastes matched those of the men all around us. She had an unimaginably large appetite for food as well as drink, and I've never seen anyone who could drink as much champagne.

I remember an orgy at the house of General Breziansko, there were about fifty guests and a couple of Grand Dukes, and when the servants had been asked to leave this young Russian, in a pure state of nature and looking like a tangled Bacchae in a frenzy, and to the unleashed joy of everyone went under the table and gave those she liked, men and women as well, the chance to show the strength and vigour of their feelings.

But I loathed this way of living in which there was no peace and quiet, and no place at all for tenderness or gentleness. Had it not been for the friend I made, she was a dancer in a restaurant, twenty-eight years old, and French, I couldn't have stayed in Russia more than a month. She was the secret mistress of the old General Breziansko, who dabbled in a kind of senile piety which was both outrageous and fragile, because he would confuse in his own way what the Gospels say about resurrection and their stories of flagellation."

Georgette, the brunette who had Elvira all in a spin with the tenderness she showed her, was a real demon when it came to lashing the leathery skin of General Breziansko. She took meticulous care over this function, and all the more so because every time her efforts were crowned with success she would get the equivalent of twenty-five thousand francs in our money. But the occurrence was a rare one, notwithstanding which the old hide Breziansko remained just as generous, and so Georgette was satisfied with her condition.

The same was not true of Elvira, who was getting thin and increasingly impatient with the encroachments of her lover and his friends on her pride. What irritated her the most was dinner at the restaurant, at the end of which there would always be some appalling row in which the waiters and the maîtres d's, mostly French, were treated in a way that revolted her, and she would seek comfort in the arms of Georgette, or by drawing flowers, little pigs and horses as well, which she would colour later and use as letterheads. They drew the admiration of Replanov who would come and see her from time to time and cry:

"She paints just like my daughter used to. I told you, Elvira, you're quite miraculously like her. That's why I'm watching over you like a father and have shown you all the best society in Russia."

Elvira escaped one day, with a bit of a heavy heart at having to leave her beautiful apartment on Pentelemonskaia. But she couldn't bear it any longer and had grown very thin. Only Georgette knew about the getaway. At the border there was another to-do, they wouldn't let her across, her passport wasn't in order. By a stroke of good fortune she caught sight of an officer on the platform she'd met in Petrograd, he ironed out all the problems and when she arrived at the Gare du Nord, Elvira only missed the strange and nostalgic songs of Russia she'd heard she couldn't remember where, in a restaurant or in the country, and the three horses as white as snow and as quick as the wind, driven with his arms stretched out by the fattest coachman in all of Russia.

George welcomed her like the prodigal son, and by the good offices of one of his friends Elvira made her music-hall debut, and that was when she started sporting a monocle. She met a little extra called Mavis Springer, her parents were wine merchants on boulevard Montparnasse, Elvira took lodgings there and found happiness in Mavis Springer, until the day a young Russian painter from a good family, Nicolas Varinov, took her away from the Springer family.

Nicolas Varinov divided his time between his sister the Princess Oettingen and his mistress Elvira, with whom he moved into a studio in rue Maison-Dieu. When Nicolas was at his sister's Elvira would paint with inventiveness, delicacy, and not a little strength of character – dazzling bouquets where buttercups would peep out with their black petals – and this life driven along by art, love, dancing at Bullier's and going to the movies went on until the outbreak of war.

1914 began wild and gay, you remember. Like in Gavarni's drawings the period was overwhelmingly one of carnival. Dance was all the fashion, everywhere people were dancing and there were masked balls everywhere. Cross-dressing was the fashion for women, and they dressed their hair in dazzling and delicate colours which reminded me of the luminous fountains that struck me so as I child when I visited the Exhibition in 1889. Or it was like the glow from the stars, and fashionable Parisian women had every right that year to be called Berenice because their hair ranked among the constellations.

 The dances at Opéra had quite naturally sprung up again, and the salacious jest at the first one where every woman was given a box and every man a key, and everyone had to find the key to their lock and the lock to their key, seemed to augur extremely well for general gaiety to come. And maybe in the years ahead, when along with the tango, the maxixe and the forlana, the war and its mortician's pomp will all have been forgotten, perhaps people will say of the year 1914, like in Gavarni's famous lithograph, that 'much will be forgiven her for the way that she danced.'

In 1914 there was no type that belonged especially to our times like The Stevedore from before, or The Domino, Pierrot and Pierrette, The Postillion, The Bayadère, Old Chicard, which a poet would swiftly have made into characters like those in Italian theatre which we would do well not to abandon.

For new masks we would need a new Gavarni.

His masterpiece was The Stevedore, especially the delightful transvestite whose nature is amply shown in the caption to a female stevedore flirting with Pierrette who's telling her to "Get away…! Strange-looking man…", which perhaps sums up the whole irreverent imagination of the 19th century.

We would also have needed a new can-can for the joyousness of those times, the old one had been brought to us by The Glutton, The Ray of Gold, Gutter-Grate and Vincent the Boneless, and by the devotion which painters such as Toulouse-Lautrec and Seurat brought to these hieratic dances of the highest order.

Something to evoke the can-can back in Gavarni's time would have been needed, a young can-can whose differences from the solemn one of the Moulin Rouge stand out quite clearly when you compare Seurat's painting *Can-can*, for example, to the much older song by Javolot and Choux that starts something like this:

> Ruckus and cancanska
> Redowa and mazurka
> My so sexy poses
> For the punters so wicked

1914, a year of dancing and fancy dress. It was a time not without its tender gravity, but a light-hearted gravity still, and there's never so much dancing as during revolutions and wars. I wonder which remarkable poet penned the common saying that's so truly prophetic, *like dancing on a volcano*?

If anyone typified those times of going to the ball and the Ballets Russes it was undoubtedly Elvira, I can still see her at Bullier's Ballroom with her lilac hair, her white furs and her monocle, she was known as The Spinning Gimlet and without any doubt that accoutrement of lilac hair, white furs and a monocle would have been everywhere the following year had it not been for the war. Perhaps another Gavarni would have emerged, and at the Opéra Ballroom we would have seen many

delightful Gimlets just like the charming Stevedores of Gavarni's time.

Sometimes Nicolas Varinov would take her to a bal-musette with Mavis: Gravilliers's, where the musicians with an accordion or a bag-pipe were up on a little balcony, and sometimes there was a barrel-organ; or Juventus on boulevard Saint-Martin, whose owner offered a lovely array of ling as a little extra for his customers; The October on rue Sainte-Geneviève, which at that time belonged to Vachier; The Balconette, which gave onto a cul-de-sac near Bastille; The Rue des Carmes Ballroom; The Songbird on rue de Vanves, and The Boules Court in Montmartre, a charming place where the music to my mind is far more pleasing than Johann Strauss.

The war assassinated all these "noble gatherings", and today Elvira still thinks of them with tenderness and melancholy.

But the war broke out and smashed like a glass this light-hearted and adorable life.

Nicolas Varinov was highly affected by this unforeseen event, and a few days after the Battle of the Marne he announced to Elvira, who had snuggled up to him like a cat, that the time for love was over for the moment, and that for him the activities involved, particularly at night, would not resume until after the end of the hostilities.

Elvira had a very ordinary interest in the war so this decision struck her as incoherent, and like a blood moon disdain began to rise in the firmament of their liaison.

Chapter Two

Sweet, fresh poetry! The most beautiful of all the arts! You give birth to our invention and bring us close to the divine, I love you with a love never cut down by the disappointments of life, you have lived with me since my earliest childhood and always will. The war has even increased the power of poetry over me, and because of war and poetry together my head broken into stars is now forever one with the sky. Sweet, fresh poetry! In these uncertain times I wish I could give myself entirely to the inspiration you bring to my subject. But the war is still on, I have to finish the book before going back and prose suits haste the best.

But even though we are at war why should we always talk of war, or the soldier's misery, or his furlough, or the miraculous sight of all the human races from all four corners of the earth mobilised at the Front, or their painful progress through the trenches?

Still, there is no forgetting this inveterate war, and no defence against remembering it. Each time I think I have escaped, it haunts me again with ever sweeter gentleness. I remember especially the instability of the soldier's life. One day he's here, perhaps that night he'll be hastening off somewhere else. Uncertainty is the lot of the infantryman especially. I have known the life of the gunner and the life of the infantryman afterwards: the instability of the infantryman is the more striking. I have heard infantrymen called Suspicion. Courageous as they are, and God knows they are courageous to the hilt, they are also suspicious because at the very least they will be asked to sacrifice their lives. But I feel nostalgic as well about this organised and nomadic existence, I remember some of the charming villages we marched through, just recently ruined, and three girls at the door of a farm-house whose roof had gone and which was now a grocery.

Today Paris draws me close. And Montparnasse, which has become to painters and poets what Montmartre was fifteen years ago – a sanctuary of simplicity, beautiful and free.

Montparnasse is wild, everyone living there agrees. The truth is that Montparnasse has replaced Montmartre, the Montmartre of before with its artists, singers, night clubs and moulins rouges, hashish eaters and the first opium maniacs, cocaine maniacs too, or visionaries as we call them now when 'coca' is still all the rage, as well as the non-stop ether-sniffers: survivors all, expelled from the old Montmartre by the carnival, from the Montmartre destroyed by developers, transformed by architects, spat upon by the Paris Futurists emigrating from there in the form of Cubists, Native Americans, and Orphic poets. Their loud voices began to infiltrate the other echoes on the corner of La Grande Chaumière. La Rotonde was open there too even before the war, the redoubtable competitor opposite, on the ground floor of a former house of ill-repute and licentious memory. The Bosch gathered over there, the Slavs were always over here. The Jews went on going to either one.

In the streets nearby the shops selling paints offer their multicoloured temptations to anyone with a passing knowledge of avant-garde exhibitions, who all seem to cry "Anch'io son pittore".

First of all, a sketch of the intersection, which more than likely will soon look very different. On the corner of the boulevard there is a large grocery with a name enigmatic enough for a whole tribe of international artists to gaze at: Chance. Merchandise of every kind, and every kind of customer. Before the war Americans would get their grapefruit there, as they call it, which is to the lemon what the melon is to the cantaloupe; Russians would stumble across their pomegranates, which look like yellow and pink cherries; Hungarians their paprika sausage, etc. And La Rotonde is on the other corner. In 1914 a Native American was the talking point, he would stand there in all his feather and  leather, like a painter and a model combined. Sometimes even the long silhouette of Charles Morice could be seen for long moments against the wall.

On the corner of boulevard Montparnasse and rue Delambre you come to Le Dôme. Before the war it thrived on its regulars, rich folk, aesthetes from Massachusetts or the banks of the river Spree, really it looks like a  painting by Pascin that's caught up with the times, or a modern-day Klingstedt. Admiration to professed in Germany later for this or that French painter was decided here. Indeed the reputations of

Géricault, Courbet and Seurat never lost out in the conversations of Bosch millionaires at Le Dôme.

Another corner now, and there's Baty, the last of the vintners. When he retires his profession will have practically disappeared from Paris, unless the war and expensive living make the guild of wine merchants fashionable again. There will still be the hole in the wall as we call it now, but those little bars will have had their time. But for now, those not forced by illness or doctors to give up French wine continue enjoying Baty's well-kept stock as much as you like.

Further along on the right, on boulevard Raspail, the tiny Daughters of the Vigorous, as it was called, used to accommodate the vivacious youth of 1914 whenever there was no dancing at Bullier. A severe looking young man was often there, and there was a simplicity about the way he used to say to anyone who would listen that "I'm the biggest pain in the arse in the neighbourhood, I even piss off the Councillors". He was known as The Lion. He pissed people off so much that he was getting a return from it, and most of the cafés and bars in the neighbourhood would give him money rather than serve him. He had just to show himself and immediately he would get a franc, two francs, or even three-fifty depending on the grandeur of the establishment. Each morning this man of genius would go on his rounds and earn enough to live, he pissed off everybody and owed nobody anything. In the provincial little Daughters of the Vigorous sometimes you would see Msrs Ségonzac, Luc-Albert Moreau, André Derain, Édouard Férat, René Dalize, and an enigmatic character called The Finn, although he was from the Limousin, in fact Limoges. The distinguished proprietor had won mint popularity in the arrondissement by declaring to everyone, carried away by his own eloquence:

"Gentlemen, even though by trade I'm a café-owner I love art, and on Sundays when I don't go the cinema I go to the Louvre."

Almost opposite there was the establishment of Mr Cocula, and in a singular moment of onomastic mimeticism, he came to deal in travel like his namesake by assonance Mr Cook. The English have the Cook travel agency, the French the Cocula railway.

In 1916, famous inhabitants of Montmartre were still living in various streets by the Montparnasse cemetery, where a bust of Édouard de Max watches over the tomb of

Baudelaire; and many including Picasso lived at the same famous address, 13 rue de Ravignan, which is now called place Émile-Goudeau.

Let's go back down rue de la Grande-Chaumière, a street full of drawing schools, where in former times, once again, the Araucanían philosopher Ortiz de Zárate, the only Patagonian in Paris, would wander up and down proclaiming he'd discovered the truth.

There was also a famous little restaurant Chez Papa frequented by models called, closed now since the beginning of the war. It was run by a one-time Garibaldian whose pasta sauces were as fine as any of the osterias of Rome. It was an enchanting place where Mr Anatole France would often have gone if he had been aware of it. Very agreeable people could be found there including Messrs Paul Morisse, André Billy, and Paul Léautaud.

Even though differently coloured from the Montmartre of before, the Montparnasse of now, even in wartime, is no less light-hearted, clear, and easy-going. The American-style clothes of the artists today are no less baggy than those of the painters and apprentices before, nor cut from a different cloth; they are simply baggy in a different way, and after all sandals are just as Germanic as the appalling elastic-sided boots we used to wear. Soon, after the war, I'll wager without wishing for it that Montparnasse will have its own night clubs, its own singers and troubadours just as it has its painters and poets now. When Bruant starts to sing about all the many different corners of this area full of fantasy and fun, the dairies, the barracks-turned-studio on rue Campagne-Première, the extraordinary Dairy-Grill on boulevard Montparnasse, the Chinese restaurant just now disappeared, the Tuesday salons at the Closerie des Lilas, gone since the war – that very day Montparnasse will have lived its time. Thomas Cook will bring convoys of travellers, the offices of the Cocula railway will emigrate to other areas of Paris and take the Chinese with it, and the Patagonians, the Comanches, the Finns from Limoges, The Daughters of Vigour and maybe even the biggest pain in the arse in the world, take them all to other destinations and another arrondissement, other hills and vales and buttes, even the Buttes Chaumont I'm sure.

During the war the exquisite and touching idea of the doll-portrait began to see the light and it deserves every bit of its success.

One of the first impressions of Paris I had when I came back wounded from the front was a scrap of phone conversation I overheard in the hospital where they were changing my bandages: "…selling those wondrous little doll portraits everywhere".

Who's talking? I never knew and it hardly matters. "That really is a bit much," I thought, "thinking about dolls at a time like this." But my opinion has changed since then. The dolls of Paris were used to show fashion all over Europe and surely that enhanced the prestige of France? Artists in Montparnasse, women artists, unsurprisingly, started using dolls as models for portraits, a charming idea which has already produced many agreeable works. If the fashion settles for these dolls our grandchildren will have some curious galleries to peer at, full of their ancestors. A performance of *Hernani* in the playroom – surely that's Grandmother in a Red Cross uniform, just like 1916 when she was young! Great-Uncle is close by, the cavalry officer with the Croix de Guerre. The young of today should not forget as the young did after 1870, and we should make more memories and more doll portraits, they are a kind of living memory.

But leave memories to one side for now, their time will come. The war goes on. Nicolas Varinov has become sombre and preoccupied. He is leaving for the front as a volunteer in a Ruthenian ambulance. His uniform, part army, part sports, is finally ready.

The evening he first wore it he went with Elvira to La Coupole on boulevard Raspail, a meeting-place for painters, models and literati. Sir Egon Allemannic was sitting outside, he was the son of a famous Austrian novelist who had conceived the singular vice of feeling constantly under threat of court action. His case was one of sexual psychopathology and I shall not go no further into it, or that of his son who, so I'm told, owes his residence permit to the favours his mother had shown a leader of one of the Opposition parties some twenty years earlier.

I would far rather paint a portrait of Moses Ladder who along with Pablo Canouris, the painter with the celestial blue hands, was reading the cards for two young Romanian women, pupils at the school of drawing nearby. Moses Ladder is a man the colour of ash whose body is musical in all its parts. He strikes his stomach and the deep tones of the cello begin to drone. From his feet he conjures the raucous rattle of a snake. When he puffs out his cheeks he has cymbals like tziganes have in restaurants, he plays his teeth with a pen and makes the crystalline sound of bottle-orchestras in a music-hall, which are also the stroke of genius on merry-go-rounds at the fair.

Elvira and Nicholas sat down at the same table and Moses shuffled the cards. Before long the Romanians went off to their drawing school, and even before they left their places were taken by Anatole Holybest, a poet and an officer wounded in the arm, coming to La Coupole for the first time since the start of the war with his new friend the lovely Coralie, red hair and hazel eyes, who taken as a whole looked like a drop of blood on the blade of a sword.

Conversation was soon very lively and turned to the subject of polygamy.

"Apparently the Bosch have legalised it," said Pablo Canouris, also known as Bluedog, "and soon we all will, I'm sure."

Lighting his pipe he went on in his heavy Spanish accent:

"If you really want to keep a wife the only way is to abduct her, lock her up and entertain her the whole time. It's hard enough to keep one woman entertained, but several – think about it! Polygamy is a theory that works for pipes, not wives."

Pablo Canouris, the painter with blue hands and the eyes of a bird. Albanian by origin he was born in Spain, in Malaga, but his heart and his brain, marked by the force of realism characteristic of Iberian Peninsular, its works and its spirit, have kept the Hellenistic purity and truth of his ancestors: for according to all those who have studied the question – Byzantine historians, Philippe de Commines, right up to Thomas Quincey and leaving aside contemporary writers – the supposed Hellenes are in fact Albanians, and the miraculous painter from Toledo, El Greco himself, was reborn in Pablo Canouris, the painter with the celestial blue hands. Not that Canouris imitated El Greco, rather the element of mystery in

 his genius touched upon that angelic violence that fills lovers of Theotocopoulos, El Greco's only son, with such delicious anxiety.

No movement since Romanticism has stirred up life as much as the new school of painting, in which only Mediterranean artists from Latin civilisations have had a part to play. Its success has given rise to a resistance from certain official quarters and an opposition to painters such as Canouris, Picasso, Braque, and Derain which is about to become still more violent than it ever was. Philosophers, it seems, have compiled a "whole arsenal of sophistry", as the song-writer Henri Delormel would say, my old friend.

But what can philosophers do against the forms and the material which are the objects studied and also the subjects chosen by the best painters of today? That the painting of today is different from the painting of yesterday, that much is obvious; but that it is out of tune with the traditions of great art, I challenge anyone to prove it. And that it places art in the slightest danger, I don't believe a word of it. The stunning, astonishing and severe studies embarked upon by the new artists are profoundly realist. Their work can never draw them away from nature, absorbed as they are in identifying and combining all the possibilities of art.

An excess of novelty? Who knows? Let me repeat, novelty is not dangerous for art but only for mediocre artists, who whatever they do will always be mediocre, and furthermore absurd, so in the end who cares! Or how absurd they are either!

So the Albanian and the Spanish were intertwined in the character of Canouris, sometimes known as Goldentail, sometimes Bluedog, sometimes Dogsprick. In appearance he was like Albanian men, many of whom are handsome, noble-looking and courageous, but with a tendency to suicide that would have you tremble for the future of their race were it not for the reproductive potency that counters their ennui. The Spanish in Bluedog had not dispelled this taste for elective death, and he had also retained a highly Albanianised Spanish liking for women.

I first knew Bluedog during a stay in Brussels, which left me with a sharp and unforgettable impression of a race which alongside the Scottish is perhaps the oldest in Europe.

Pablo Bluedog lived there before Paris and had gone straight there from Malaga. An English woman was his girlfriend and she made him suffer as only those who belong to humanity's elite can suffer in love.

This young woman had an insolent beauty, any man would have been driven mad with love for her, and she was unfaithful to my friend with anyone kind enough to oblige. And I myself, may I be forgiven, deliberated long and hard about the respective demands of friendship and desire.

Shameless in a way that those abused by life, cross-eyed in the soul and one-eyed in the heart cannot fail to admire, Maud spent her time in the studio of my friend with her clothes off, and whenever Pablo went out debauchery came in.

And so this Maud, what was her place in humanity?

She spoke none of its languages but a hybrid dialect, a mixture of English and French with Belgian and German turns of phrase.

A philologist would have adored her, a grammarian could only have detested her regardless of her beauty.

Her father was English, an officer whose cruelty saw him condemned to death in India for brutality against indigenous people. But her mother was Maltese.

One day my friend said to me:

"I've got to be free. I'm going to kill myself tomorrow."

I knew Pablo Bluedog's character well enough to know these words were not spoken in vain.

He would certainly kill himself since he said he would.

I never left his side, as a result of which, and my friendship as well, in the following days Pablo Bluedog did not kill himself.

He found a remedy by himself for this torment.

"This woman," he said, "is not my wife. It's true I love her, but a spouse would have wiped that love from my soul."

"I don't understand! Explain yourself!" I cried.

He smiled and went on in his heavy Spanish accent:

"The people of the Balkans and in the mountains of the Adriatic used to practice abduction, and the custom continues in various localities. Only a woman we've taken really belongs to us, a woman we've tamed. Without abduction there can be no happy marriage. I courted Maud, but she's the one who took me. She's free and I want to conquer my own freedom again."

"How?" I asked in surprise.

"Abduction," he said in a tone of calmness and nobility that impressed me no little.

The following days Pablo and I went travelling.

He took me to Holland and for a few days he appeared very anxious.

I wanted to respect his pain and with thoughts of abduction seemingly out of the way, I silently praised him for using absence to help him forget his Maud, who had put him in such a fever that he wanted to take his own life.

In Amsterdam one morning, Bluedog pointed out a girl walking along Kalverstraat beside her governess, with her music rolled up under her arm.

A valet in quality livery walked ten yards behind the two women.

The young girl might have been seventeen years old. Her hair was tied in two plaits down her back.

She was the daughter of a patrician Amsterdam family, and she seemed as light-hearted as Holland can only ever be in the Athens of Batavia.

"Follow me," Bluedog suddenly said.

He started running and quickly overtaking the servant he picked the young girl up by the waist and ran off faster still.

Fit to explode I ran in high anxiety after my friend.

I never looked back but clearly the bewildered governess and valet had lost their heads, and not a single cry of "Stop thief" was to be heard from them!

We arrived at the train station.

The young woman smiled in fascination at the poise and manhood of her abductor, ravishing in every sense, and when we were on the train to Rosendaël, towards the border, Pablo Canouris, the painter with the azure hands, began to kiss this most submissive of fiancées to the outer reaches of his soul.

She died two months later. And this time I thought I would never be able to prevent the suicide of my friend.

But I succeeded in bringing him to Paris where he settled, and it would take too long to go into the detail of all his loves in the capital. Suffice it to say that on this particular day he had been single for a couple of weeks.

"Tomorrow I'm leaving for the war," said Nicolas Varinov to Pablo Canouris, sometimes known as Dickdog, "would you please take Elvira to the cinema this evening? The programme changes on a Friday, and she's inconsolable if she misses the new one, even for one week. I've quite a number of errands to run myself, and this evening I'll be dining with my family at my sister's."

After a short while he got up and left with a worried look, lost in thoughts of the war. He said goodbye to Elvira, who watched her lover with a heavy heart as he walked away without once looking back.

In that moment a sergeant who, rumour had it, was a German called Winkheimer, but who had in fact got himself into the Foreign Legion as an Alsatian enlisting under the name Ovid St-Euxine, came up to the table. He was convalescing from a wound.

As soon as he saw Elvira he cried: "Didn't you once tell me your grand-mother had been a Mormon?"

"Yes," Elvira replied, "and I'm sure that's why I'm not jealous. My lover can have as many mistresses as he likes, I'd feel just the same as a Mormon about her wife-sisters. My parents often told me the story of my grandmother Pamela's escapade. But the one who really enlightened me about her was a kind of library rat, a Bosch who'd once been Drekheim's secretary, he was another Bosch and he'd written a history of Mormonism. Drekheim had been to the capital of the Mormons in 1895, and in 1908 he sent this Firpnitz character there, he was in love with me in Petrograd where he'd been some sort of secretary for Replinov. He was always talking about the Mormons so I brought out the story of my grandmother again. He was absolutely fascinated, and in his papers he found the copy he'd made in Salt Lake City of a letter written by a famous Mormon, the same Mormon who'd converted my grandmother, and he talks about her. Firpnitz translated the letter for me and gave it to me to read."

"Well, since the war," the pseudo Ovid St-Euxine rejoined, "I'm in touch again with one of my great-uncles, he says he's from Strasbourg but maybe he came to France from Hesse in '66, because even in times of war, the Guelphs have never had anything to fear from the French. But anyway, even before the war I knew my great-uncle existed but I never went to see him. Since the war he's been very kind to me and I always stay with him when I'm on leave. As a young boy he went to Utah with his mother, she was a widow, and she was carried along on one of the first convoys of new faithfuls from Europe. Otto Warning, my great uncle, spent his childhood there and only came back to his native country at the age of twenty-five, where he married in the European way. But ever since I've been seeing him he talks about nothing but Mormonism. He's always coming back to it, he says it's the way to give France the rise in population it needs to stay a great nation."

"But do you think it's useful to bring many children into the world?" asked Elvira.

"Useful? In fifty years there'll be a hundred million Bosch, and sixty million Italians, I'll spare you the Spanish and all the other nations that surround us, and France by then won't even have reached its forty-first million yet, at this rate."

"It'd be fun if your great-uncle knew by grandmother," said Elvira.

"Exactly," said Ovid, "I promised him you'd go and see him. It's close by, rue Delambre, I'll give you the address."

"Good," said Elvira, "You can expect me at about three. I'll bring the letter. It's dated 1851."

"Marvellous!" cried Ovid. "I do think Great-Uncle Otto was there. Anyway see you tomorrow!"

And as it was dinner time Pablo Bluedog took her to the jernt that was fashionable in the area.

In the artists' milieu the word "bistrot" is no longer used, "taproom" has no longer existed for a while now either, the word died away with the Symbolists and the last person I heard using it was Remy de Gourmont. Nowadays people just say "Let's go to Mildred's, it's a yummy little jernt."

And bistrot will be relegated to the attic of period words soon to be poetic, like topcoat, tart, hansom cab, the victoria, the banger, etc., etc., with which poets a hundred years from now will decorate poems that are supposed to evoke our times: like Verlaine putting words into *Les Fêtes Galantes* that he thinks best evoke the eighteenth century.

After dinner at the cinema, and as Pablo Goldentail was watching the screen with no other thought in his mind, he suddenly felt a little hand in his hands. He was shaken all over and a sort of lust mixed with horror came over him. But slowly his hand began to squeeze Elvira's.

Chapter Three

Nicolas Varinov had left with an absent-minded kiss for Elvira, and Elvira had returned it with a still more absent-minded one of her own. He was thinking about the communiqué, she was thinking about the cinema.

What a strange thing it was that a woman like Elvira with a man's liking for women should have such a mad crush on Nicolas Varinov. Certainly it was far from ruined, but rather it was falling away, given all the uncertainties that had arisen since the war, in addition to which he seemed no longer to have any thoughts of love. She found Pablo Canouris attractive, also known as Pablo Goldentail, and as he was from a neutral country his fate seemed less uncertain than that of Nicolas. His budding fame moreover meant his friendship would guarantee the success of a painter from within his circle such as herself, and not without talent either. Elvira was more of a painter than she even knew. But her thoughts were not turning to Pablo Canouris or the intertwining of their hands. She was remembering various scenes from other films that had charmed her, alongside the conversation with Ovid that had touched on Mormonism.

She wondered as she got ready to go to rue Delambre, looking for the letter where her grandmother was mentioned:

"After all, I don't see why there shouldn't be a female Mormonism or women with several husbands. That would be fun. And for lovers if not husbands it already exists anyway. I'll have to do a portrait of Anatole Holybest in his lieutenant's uniform and with his new Coralie. But she'll be hard to draw, that one."

Then she went off to the meeting in rue Delambre. The old Hessian who had lived with the Mormons was a handsome old man with a clear and open-minded intelligence. His words of welcome were these:

"I certainly knew your grandmother in 1851. I was eight when I arrived in Salt Lake City, in August that year. Read me the letter out loud, I can't read handwriting any more, even with my glasses."

And while pseudo-Ovid St-Euxine tore the cuticles from his nails and old man Warning opened his mouth the better to hear, closing it now and then to take a pinch of snuff, Elvira unfolded the letter Firpnitz had copied for her in Petrograd, and read it aloud at a steady pace and with the dignity only to be expected of a young woman once a familiar at the Folies-Bergères.

> *To Brother Brigham Young*
> *President of The True and Living Church of the Latter-Day Saints*
> *Governor of the Territory of Utah*
> *Great Salt Lake City*
> *United States of America*[1]

Paris, 20 December, 1851

I believe I shall be the first, Brother Brigham Young, to inform you of the tragic events that have put Paris to the fire and the sword, the unfortunate capital of France. However in the event that the news has preceded this letter, let me reassure you of my own fate and that of the mission.

When, in conformity with the wishes of the Church Council, I bade farewell to my wives and left Salt Lake City to lead the mission charged with proselytising in Old Europe, nothing could have prepared me for the astonishment, the admiration, as well as the horror that lay in wait for me in the giant city that has taken the place of Rome at the centre of the world.

There reigns in Paris a singular mixture of splendour and poverty that cannot fail to strike a citizen of the United States, accustomed as we are to the pleasing simplicity of our blossoming cities which, while lacking the sublime architecture of palaces, monuments and religious edifices, the grandiose arrangement of squares and gardens, the vistas from promenades fashioned with such delicacy and audacity, are also without the most dreadful filth to be found in the suburbs of Paris, and the appalling houses in which workers and petits bourgeois alike are nauseatingly piled together cheek by jowl.

In these narrow and tortuous streets, the smell of rot battles with the fetid urine that soils the whole of Paris, stagnating in puddles, frothing in

---

[1] *Author's Note*: I publish Mr Taylor's letter with all the curious annotations to be found on the translation in Elvira's possession, and which she has allowed me to include as part of her permission to publish.

the gutters, and joining the stink of human faeces mixed with animal.

I have never missed anywhere in Europe as much as I have in Paris what we have come to know as the honest savagery of our lands.

The pock-marked façades that bear witness to the many revolutions look like old women, like squaws worn out by life and the ill-treatment of wives common amongst the Red Skins, the wretched remnants of the wretched Lamanites.

Moreover here as everywhere in Europe nature is meaner than in our native land, the rivers in particular are like meagre creeks compared to our Missouri, the Father of all Waters, and our other American rivers.

I arrived in Paris in April from Copenhagen, where I had the good fortune to garner a number of Danish proselytes, whom you have no doubt have had the joy by now of welcoming to our Holy City.

Having visited Paris on many occasions I knew how hard was the life of our brother Curtis Bolton, charged with the difficult task of converting the Parisians. In spite of many obstacles he succeeded in concluding four hundred conversions, even though I must say his circumstances served him very poorly indeed.

For several years he lived in an attic in rue Tournon, and despite his best efforts he rarely earned more ten francs a month, on which he could only live on bread and water.[2]

I thought it time for him to rest, and immediately upon my arrival I took upon myself, being sufficiently familiar with the French language, the task of bringing to fruition his translation of the Book of Mormon.

This work will in all likelihood appear in the course of next year.

I sent Brother Curtis Bolton to England and to people of his own race, who welcomed him warmly; and from his enthusiastic letters I know that his apostolate gave rise to many a dance. You know how agreeable dances are to the gods, concerts and excursions as well, and also garden parties with the most agreeable games.

Did he not go to Jersey with a small troupe of Saints and young women about to become our sisters? During this delightful journey there was nothing but preaching, canticle singing, and the fulfilment of carnal desire according to human and divine law, which requires polygyny,

---

[2] America had not yet discovered the skyscraper, and nowadays Mr Taylor would have been surprised by the small number of floors in Paris houses. As to rue Tournon, I know it well, it is well located and its population is an honourable one. (*Recent, anonymous note made by a reader in the Salt Lake City public library, perhaps the Keeper of Manuscripts.*)

following the example of the patriarchs and of Christ himself, who had three spouses as the Gospels show.

Brother Curtis Bolton's vacation is now over, and filled with zeal he is preparing his return to Paris.

Once the apostle has returned, I shall leave France to visit our missions in Italy.

But here are some further details of my stay in Paris.

Upon my arrival I took lodgings at 27 rue Paradis-Poissonnière, which is both densely populated and gloomy and which by force of habit I have begun to like, although I am still affected by the foul-smelling air in my room, which is very close to the street, as is common in a large number of houses in Paris.

What pity can only be felt, even by the hardest of hearts, at the misfortunes the people of Paris have had to endure! The rapid succession of riots and revolutions hardly gives these wretched people the time to recover from war and slaughter.

The gods know how much we of the Church of the Latter-Day Saints are accustomed to riots. One of them cost our prophet Joseph Smith his life, and that of his brother the patriarch Hyrum, in the prison at Carthage. I was there myself and badly wounded. Nauvoo, The Beautiful City, which we built with our own hands, was seized from us by the Gentiles, many of our congregation were martyred and the Temple was sacked. But nothing can give an idea of the desperate look of Paris I discovered when I arrived in April this year. The remnants of barricades, the ruins from the fires, the memories of revolution and war and the battered victims of both, it all made me think that our trials and tribulations in search of Deseret which you promised us, and which we found, and named after the little supernatural honeybee in accordance with a revelation that came to you, are like no more than sweet recreation compared to the woes of all kinds which political fury and a misunderstood love for the least democratic of all freedoms have brought upon the French in just a few years, especially the Parisians.

I felt this desolation was soon to run its course, and assuming my apostolate, following the excellent state in which brother Curtis Bolton had left his own, I was able to baptise a few French men at 282 rue Saint-Honoré. I founded a newspaper, *The Star of Deseret*, to support my preaching, following the example of the Prophet Joseph Smith as well as your own, our new Prophet. As of May the broadsheet is published weekly, and I know you will approve of its title.

Since the police continues to harass me as it harassed, or rather persecuted our poor brother Curtis Bolton, I resolved not to discuss anything in the newspaper connected to politics. One of the new saints, brother Dupont, a witness to one of my miracles, appears to me now as a very ordinary poet in truth, but in the hope of better to come the few canticles he has composed in French do serve a purpose. He helped brother Bolton with his translation of *The Book of Mormon* and he is helping me now by correcting typographical errors on the proofs.

Do I need to say that I remain silent on the element of our doctrine which is so appealing to young men, namely polygamy?

From the very beginning of my apostolate I feared that the superficial and sarcastic character of the French would lead them to pour scorn on our Church, should the ritual of patriarchy required in our families be widely known.

One of the reputedly classic authors of this country, Mr Molière, who two centuries ago wrote some priceless pieces of buffoonery, composed verses for a play I saw recently at the Théâtre-Français which scandalised me, although they seemed very funny and perfectly attuned to the Parisian audience who laughed immoderately, and which would sound like a legally-binding ruling to our Gentiles of Illinois (or illegal as you will, never forgetting our Judge Lynch, that manifestation of pure injustice), as well as the Gentiles of the Washington Congress and the United States army.

Here are Mr Molière's verses, worthy of the uncivilised vagabonds, mercenaries and the roughest cowboys of our savage Far West:

> Polygamy is a hanging
> Is a hanging offence.

A cruel and inhuman ditty, which might have been composed in America with us directly in mind, but the recollection of them here is enough to destroy us forever in the minds of the French, who would then treat us as the dissolute horde they are themselves.

Moreover polygamy already exists here, as matter of reality and in the form of debauchery, as I have just intimated.

Marriage in France, while legally monogamous is often, in truth, and as it were openly, polygamous, both for the husband and the spouse, by the means of adultery, which in this country is a once a serious and laughable act, and not infrequently the ridicule it attracts becomes fatal.

Even so, while polygamy is no longer a hanging offence at the discretion of the law, and while the humour of the verses quoted above belongs to the jester and not the gallows, polygamy is nonetheless suppressed by French law when sanctioned by a ritual or legal act; and my desire to avoid serious disputes with the police is consistent with my desire to pursue the triumph of our Church of the Latter-Day Saints, since the expulsion of our Apostles from the country would certainly decimate the small kernel of believers created by the zeal, previously noted, of brother Curtis Bolton.[3]

This having been said let me turn to the events of the last days, and the large number of people who lost their lives convinces me I was within an inch of my own.

My determination not to get involved in politics and to avoid giving opinions that might be misinterpreted should letters be intercepted, which the police is currently doing, it seems, and with good reason, prevents me from communicating my ideas on the cause of these events, but I wish nonetheless to recount them, without passing any judgement. The riots and revolutions, from which Paris was still in such turmoil when I arrived in April, began again as a result of a certain governmental action known as the Coup d'État. Suffice it to add by way of explanation that the President of the Republic, who belongs to the Bonaparte family, is planning a return in his own favour of Imperial pomp. He began with a show of absolutism which offended a considerable number of people from all classes, and workers especially.

Following the advice I had been given I remained indoors on the 2nd as well as the 3rd of December. But on the 4th I had to go to our printer in rue Saint-Benoît on the left bank of the Seine, and though a hardened

---

[3] The late Mr Drekheim, the scholar from Berlin who for five years lived in Salt Lake City, consulting the papers bequeathed to the Library by the lamented President Brigham Young, took the liberty of asking Mr Taylor, still alive then, the reason why, since he feared the police would read his letters, he spoke at such length in them about polygamy. To which Mr Taylor replied that he had done so consciously so that the police would believe there was no discussion of multiple wives in *The Star of Deseret*, and not a word of it in the sermons either. He added that for that matter, educated people and functionaries in the police would have already known that the Mormons of Utah were polygamous. *(A note written in pencil in the margin of the letter.)*

Later in the letter Mr Taylor shows his fear of the infamous black office, where there must indeed have been a lot to do if all the post was being opened. *(A note written in ink in a woman's hand under the one above.)*

traveller there was no recovering from my astonishment at the brutality of the soldiers. Taking a detour I came upon rue de la Paix where I saws lancers, which are soldiers in the cavalry, charging a crowd of well-dressed people, chamber-maids and children of the well-to-do.

Nonetheless I was able to take cover and avoid being trampled underfoot by the horses, but coming back from rue Saint-Benoît I made the mistake of going a way I thought would be shorter, and found myself wandering from barricade to barricade: I would find it difficult now to reconstruct my itinerary through the maze of streets transformed by the barricades into makeshift citadels.

The morality of European nations is so different from the one which prevails amongst Americans that I cannot say whether you will understand the motivation behind the internecine struggles that divide the French. Nothing is truly democratic here. The Equality emblazoned on the facades of public buildings is in reality wished for by none of the social classes.[4]

At home everything derives from the people: religion, art, power, and wealth. The American nation is a ladder whose rungs are equal and show only the differences in elevation, and this holds true in the spiritual world as much as the material one. From time to time the ladder is turned upside down but nothing is changed.

In France instead of a single ladder there are many, each climbing the same mountain. Or to say it more directly, each class forms its own State within the nation, with its own aristocracy, its own bourgeoisie and its own plebs. The arts are organised in this guise as well, and the democratic unity so admired in us is nowhere to be seen. Science and the trades are organised according to this system, and the science of war us understood in the same way as well. By an extraordinary turn of events, the science of fortifications has produced a plebeian form of the barricade, and while the learned military parade all the instruction handed down to them from Italian engineers of the 15th century, and while they continue to apply their expertise to perfecting fortifications, the people have invented the barricade, which is an unplanned and makeshift fortress made of paving stones, pillars

---

[4] This missionary, however keen an observer, knows nothing of human nature, since there is no class in any nation that desires equality. The terminology of legislators and politicians is often in conflict with human nature and the human passions, which demand the following order of things: to each his own strength, right, and the fruits of his own labour. (*This observation written in pencil in the margin of the letter was probably made by the Emperor of Brazil, don Pedro, at the time of his visit to Salt Lake City.*)

and posts, barrels, overturned omnibuses, baskets and mattresses. These ramparts sometimes reach as high as a second storey, and on occasion these shapeless and disparate piles of debris have had the better of regular soldiers and artillery.

At home the people are the whole-world: millionaires, farmers, journalists, speculators, livestock traders: exception is only made of shepherds, Negroes and Indians, the latter are the blessèd enemy that we supplant on their own soil, and the others are not part of humanity.

Here the people are made only of criminals, the poor, workers, students, representatives, artists and men of letters. And often there a terrible outbreaks of fury. The government has the measure of them, but blood flows abundantly.

I will not describe in detail the barricades I came upon on the 4th of this month as I struggled back to my lodgings. You are not familiar with the typography of Paris, and such explanations would be of no value to you. Suffice it to say that along rue Rambuteau alone, which I was obliged to go down even though it was out of my way, I counted up to twelve barricades.

Elsewhere, in front of a large barricade blocking rue Saint-Denis at the corner of rue Guérin-Boisseau, I was taken for an informer, "un mouchard" as they commonly say.[5] I was not very happy, and in spite of being American which I attempted in vain to explain, the rioters would have shot me had it not been for the intervention of the representative Victor Hugo, celebrated as a poet. He questioned me, and after asking at length about Niagara Falls, the use of stilts in Mexico, the customs of the Osage people and the course of the Orinoco River, he had me released; and with the rioters listening respectfully he addressed me in words which I quote verbatim here: "Wise citizen of the United States of America, bear witness tomorrow in your free Republic to the struggles today of the Titanic people of Paris, who will soon be cementing the United States of Europe."

Whereupon shaking both my hands he took his leave, and I was locked in a pharmacy which the rioters had transformed into a powder factory.

According Mr Daniele Manin, President of Venice, who visited me about three months ago curious to know all things Mormon, this Mr Victor Hugo was living as much as possible here in Paris and according

---

[5] Author's note: the French word is used in the original letter.

the accepted principles of our Church, particularly with regard to polygamy, and without creating a scandal.

After a few moments which to me seemed never-ending I was allowed on my way. Barricade after barricade, stepping over the dead and the wounded and avoiding the bayonets and the projectiles of the soldiers, I arrived I could not say how on the "boulevart" where the butchery was horrible to behold.[6]

The soldiers were massacring everyone they saw, and the cries of "Murderers!", "Down with Bonaparte!", "Long Live the Republic!" mixed in a terrifying music with the officers' orders, the wails of the dying, the rattle of gunfire and the thunder of the canon. I thought my end could well be nigh and my first thought was to take refuge in a shop, but they were mostly closed, and from the shopkeepers' corpses in the ones still open I soon saw there would be no refuge from the soldiers anywhere.

It had started to rain and the mud that had formed in places began to mix with the blood. Stragglers hurried past, rioters trying to reach their barricades, some crouching to avoid the projectiles, others hurled insults at the armed forces, proudly and defiantly. They were not there long though, anxious to be gone before the arrival of the soldiers, two companies of which were approaching from opposite directions. I was sure I would never escape them and prepared to meet my death. But in that moment a group of young, elegantly turned-out men and women passed me by, laughing as they went. They seemed very unconcerned by the riot as though sheltered from all danger, and it occurred to me to follow them, but still laughing and joking they turned and drove me away with their walking-sticks. "On your way, little man, the likes of you don't belong with us," the dissolute lot cried, for dissolute they were, and debauched.

One of the women turned back, she picked up a bottle lying next to a dead soldier and a shako, and hurled it at me: "Hurry up Pamela! And stay away from that socialist!"

The bottle hit me on the forehead and dazed me, wounding me above the right eye. Straightaway I heard a soft voice saying:

"Poor man, you're bleeding."

And then close to me there was a rustle of silk, and a delicate hand staunched the blood from my wound with a scented handkerchief.

---

[6] Author's note: the French word with its obsolete spelling is the one used in the original letter.

At first I thought it was our Angel Moroni appearing on the battle field to save one of the faithful of John Smith. But this pitilessly debauched group hurrying on this day of sorrow towards the next tavern, Au Rocher de Cancale or some other, to feast on oysters and the suffering of the people, shouting "Come on, Pamela, the soldiers are coming!", soon gave me to understand that there was no Angel Moroni by my side, only Pamela lagging behind, to whom her friends were calling with all their arrogance and without any danger to themselves, nor coming to fetch her either from this dangerous place, where she had voluntarily stayed to help me. The battalions were running up in a rhythmical charge, and the even sound of their boots approached in a sinister dance macabre.

The angel Pamela was unconcerned and I thought I would die at her side. This novelistic demise inspired me for a moment, and I thought that when the bayonets came I would cry "Long Live the Republic!", which coming from me would be a legitimate celebration of our United States, but which to the soldiers about to become my executioners (a capital piece of the gallows humour on the spur of the moment) would sound like a defence *in extremis* of the people's regime they were seeking to suppress.

But the hand that wiped my face took me away by the arm, I could make out the military uniforms mixed with the angelic shape of the woman who had come to my rescue, in her other hand she held the handkerchief stained with my blood and it reminded me of Christ and Saint Veronica. This edifying thought filled my mind the whole time we crossed the "boulevart" and down an adjacent street, just in time to avoid falling prey to the soldiers.

Brother Brigham, such was my, so to speak, miraculous escape from the disciplined fury of the military; and please excuse the digression on the subject of French women which now follows.

They could be described in the same way as I once wrote to you about Catholic priests, who are worth more than the priests of any other religion, and other than in our own Church you will find no greater number of Saints anywhere. There is nothing surprising in that, since Catholicism is the one true religion after Judaism, and was the repository of truth until the angel Moroni appeared to Joseph Smith. And I have often been enchanted by the truths the Catholic priests try so hard to propagate with a courage and a good will beyond words.

The same goes for the women of France, they are excellent in health, willingness to work, courage, gentleness, grace, good taste and good humour; and those who depart from the restraint that befits the fair sex are led astray more by institutional vice than their own inclinations.

Nowhere other than here would polygamy be more useful, where people have completely lost sight of the notion of marriage. For many socialists freedom in love is an indisputable right, and polygamy whether married or unmarried is accepted as valid even by Fourier in proposing his eminently immoral Bayaderism.

Polygamy gives health to man as well as woman, it eliminates prostitution and its attendant miseries and illnesses, it increases the majesty of man and satisfies his innate desire for dominance. Constitutional patriarchy would suit this country perfectly, and even resolve the problem of society by eliminating those internecine struggles and morbid ideologies that impoverish both mind and body. If not that, then what else but the adultery of clandestine polygamy, the prostitution that comes from turning carnal relation into something shameful, destroying in the process man's pleasure in procreation and leading men to folly, covering the earth with wretched children devoid of family and prospects and doomed to contempt for their illegitimacy.

The woman who had led me away urged me to keep running. Finally we came to a house, I followed my saviour into an elegant apartment where having graciously shown me in, she said:

"My father and my brother are both workers, and fighting against tyranny. That's why I was so moved when I saw that big coward Berthe hit you with a bottle. I immediately decided to save you. You're a representative, aren't you?"

I explained my status as an American and a Mormon missionary, whereupon she expressed keen interest:

"I was raised as a daughter of Mary…. Those were the good times."

I understood that the young woman was living in a state of perdition

and that she recalled the days of her innocence with sadness. I thought straightaway she would make an excellent Mormon, and that French women being so rare amongst the Saints, you would be pleased to have amongst you a female specimen of the ingenious French race, to which civilisation in all its aspects owes so much. I began to indoctrinate this grisette and returned every day to Bréda where she lived in the 9th arrondissement. I showed her that joy and happiness awaited her in Salt Lake City, that we were the repositories of the true doctrine, that she would have a pleasing husband, that Mormon women are educated and well brought-up, that we like dances, music and theatre, and that we do everything to keep up with Paris fashion so that as a Parisian, her taste would rank her above all her sisters in these matters. Anyway, whether with regard to marriage or the luxury of our lives I had the ear of Madam Pamela, as she mentally shuffled her regrets like cards in her mind. I discovered she asked the woman who minds the street door for advice, and that she strongly opposed my plan. Other women friends of Pamela also argued against listening to me, but she had the good sense to ask her father's opinion, a well-respected worker less known in his working-class suburb by his real name Monsenergues than by the moniker King Paris of Love. This worthy gentleman came over to his daughter's and exhorted her to follow virtue. He rued the day he had failed to immolate his daughter, when led astray by pleasure and luxury she had escaped from paternal authority and chosen a life of perdition.

Tears came to my eyes as I listened to this rugged and sensitive man, whose hands covered in calluses would make gestures like caresses in the air.

When he heard what I was advising he became very enthusiastic, spoke in praise of what he knew of the United States, Champ d'Asile in Texas, and generals of the ilk of Cincinnatus. He urged his daughter to take my advice. Deploring the political events of the moment in which he was entangled, he was outraged that the forces of tyranny had banished a man he held in high esteem, a certain Agricol Perdiguier, otherwise known as Avignon-the-Virtuous.

Upon this exchange Pamela Monsenergues made up her mind. She packed her bags, sold or gave away everything that would get in the way during the voyage or on arrival, and I have the pleasure to inform you that this young woman has decided to join a group of other young Saints soon to depart for America under the leadership of brother Lorenzo Snow. There will also be a number of English women, Danish and Norwegian as well, one other French woman, and a whole family of Swiss. Brother Lorenzo, who brings a new wife to his home in Salt Lake City, took the decision himself to escort the caravan.

I am sorry not to be able to send more French women. But you will settle I know for the herd of heifers I am steering over to you, the powerful bulls in our sacred stables will take delight in fertilising them, and the precious domain that the gods have entrusted to you for protection will grow in peace and in happiness, brother Brigham, our prophet.

To conclude this letter, I am bound to inform you that an Anglican priest is trying in vain to give the lie to the ethnic truths we hold dear, that form the basis of our religion, and that for centuries have been proclaimed by Catholic writers, keepers of all truth until the Angel Moroni appeared to Joseph Smith. During his voyage in Asia this priest arrived amongst the Nestorians, and maintains they are the lost descendants of the ten tribes of Israel whose traces were lost in history until the day The Book of Mormon proved that having emigrated to America, there is now a small portion left of one of those tribes, the Lamanites, Jews punished by God but nonetheless the last representatives of his people: I mean the red race which we respect. This book full of bad faith makes no mention of our truths, and its publication was another moment when I saw the infernal ignorance, the brazen and evil insolence of sects spread all over the earth by the forces of iniquity. Catholic priests by contrast have known the truth by revelation, before the complete revelation of the Golden Plates to Joseph Smith, who admired Catholicism greatly. They live in dignity, selflessness and holiness. They were the keepers of truth, our Church is merely the continuation of Catholicism, and has adapted to the new revelations.

I call upon your solicitude with regard to my home, and following one of the revelations I ask you not to hesitate in presenting a replacement to my wives, should that become necessary during my absence.

With my deepest respect, I remain your

Brother John Taylor, martyr."

Elvira stopped and looked questioningly at so-called St-Euxine, still tearing his cuticles from his fingers and making them bleed, and at old Warning who said: "I remember the martyr John Taylor perfectly, and Lorenzo Snow, and your grandmother Pamela. If you have the time I can recall her story. You'll not hear it from anyone other than me.

I was a child then, but children mixed together with great freedom. We observed, and we were far from innocent. My mother who died there was one of the eleven wives of Robin Formesnear, but it isn't the story of my mother you want to hear but the story of your grandmother, Pamela. Listen carefully, but tell me if you get tired. I'm never brief and I'm always pleased to talk at length about this intriguing subject, I'm so rarely given the chance."

"Agreed," said Elvira. "Tell me everything you know about my grandmother. I think she must have looked like me."

"That's true," replied Otto, looking at her lengthily. "But she looked sullen and insolent as well, whereas you look more withdrawn."

"I love her already," cried Elvira, "and how lucky she was to live in a time so full of surprises."

"I wouldn't complain, if I were you, when it comes to surprises I think you've been well served, what with Russia, grand-dukes, painting and the war! What more would you want?"

"That's not the same," was Elvira's response, "and as amazing as that may seem my life is still very down to earth."

"You're very hard to please!" St Euxine concluded. "You should learn how to savour your existence."

And he turned to the old man, inviting him to begin.

Chapter Four

"It was in Utah," began old Otto Warning, "on the main square in the centre of Salt Lake City, at about three in the afternoon. At first the caravan came into view like puffs of gun smoke, which formed into many little black dots emerging on the horizon, and began to snake towards us like a procession of ants. The train quickly grew larger, and close to the canvas-covered wagons and the carts, the women and men on foot carrying heavy loads, armed men on horseback began to appear, and soon we could hear the cries of the people, the grinding of the wheels and the whinnying of the horses.

One after another, at irregular intervals and in disordered groups, foot-travellers, riders and teams of livestock were arriving in the capital of The Latter-Day Saints.

After five months at sea, without sight of land other than the forbidding rocks of Cape Horn, a troupe of emigrants had reached California to join the adepts of polygamy in America. They had made the hard journey across the great salt desert and everyone, the men and the women, dismounting their horses and clambering from their wagons, sat and looked at the amphitheatre of the city built on the slopes of the Wasatch Mountains, whose eternally white snow-peaks that day were delicately coloured in tender pinks and pale greens. Everyone, the dusty travellers, the thin and drawn anxious young girls, waited quietly for the apostle Lorenzo Snow, at that moment making his visit to the Prophet, and exhaustion silenced them all.

Wide streets led away from the main square, and along them at regular intervals quadrangular wooden houses nestled in orchards filled with apricot and peach trees covered in fruit.

Around the square elegant milliners, instrument-makers, seed-merchants and tobacco-merchants, alcohol, foodstuffs, agricultural tools – merchants of all kinds were advertising their wares with multicoloured signs, most of which figured an eye painted in blue to show the trader was Mormon.

There were also money changers and their stalls, and in violet pots in front of the hotel little orange trees looked like a Mappa Mundi ringed with leaves.

Soon all the shopkeepers were on their doorsteps the better to examine the emigrants. Some smoked their pipes, others chewed tobacco, from time to time sending a long trail of bronze-coloured saliva onto the ground, and some were carefully whittling a piece of wood in their left hand with a penknife they held in their right.

Gradually children began to cluster around the new arrivals and the little boys, thin and nasty looking, took the hands of little girls, put their arms around their waists and kissed them brazenly, laughing all the while and pointing at the travellers. One of the little girls was smoking a cigarette, she took it away from her mouth with each puff and let the smoke out with her eyes closed. These were the first generation of children in the burgeoning city.

Cities! Cities, you're the most sublime of monuments to human Art. The indefinite movement of human life rises to an infinite immobility. Weariness has us wish for the active repose of the vegetable world. Nomads pause for a moment, and standing in a row like trees in a forest they begin to plant their spiritual roots, houses being to surface, and a town to cast its shadows. And the wondrous unity of the new foundation emerges, with its towers and dwellings, its aqueducts and sewers, its architects and its pontiffs, all in the name of the City.

The children were playing in the sun and no sense of modesty had been imposed upon them. They lived in a society where religion honours and commends the work of the flesh, and their appetites were lauded by the seraglios of their fathers.

Three Amerindians walked proudly out of a saloon. They were Utes dressed in old trousers and fur hats, they had precious moccasins on their feet decorated with white and green beads, and red bandanas were knotted at their necks. They walked along with great dignity, in the full knowledge they were respected as a last remnant of the Lamanites, the last descendants of the ten tribes of Israel lost after the fall of Babylon, and whose history of greatness and disaster on the continent of America is contained in the Book of Mormon.

Because of their origin they constituted the nobility of the new city, where they were allowed to live in the foulest poverty and debauchery.

And their traditions, which they continued to follow in spite of their moral decay, had been the model of Mormon reform.

Suddenly there was intense life on the main square. The caravan all stood up and the few men moved away to join the throng flooding the square from everywhere. Only the women remained by the wagons, talking amongst themselves, brushing each other down, coquettishly combing their hair to show off their advantages. English women looking good in Mexican trousers, wide at the bottom and with leather fringes along the stitching. Danish and Norwegian women, too modest to wear men's clothes. They looked pretentious and pathetic in their showy skirts, the colours had faded in the voyage, the ruffles had torn and the crinoline-covered hoops were broken. A young Swiss one looked even more ridiculous in her finery from before 1848, and with a microscopic bibi-bonnet on her head. But there was one, the very one that interests you, Elvira, your grandmother Pamela, who didn't seem at all concerned about her appearance. She was dressed in the clothes of a sailor, with a beret and uncombed hair, and she stared boldly at the multitudes gathering on the square, which seemed to form two groups neither of which showed any wish to mingle, in spite of the commotion of the children running around between them.

The Amerindians sat in the middle of the square, and instead of tobacco which they scorned smoked their kinnikinnick in precious pipes made of red clay.

Soon people in long white robes stood by them, they had papal tiaras on their heads, also white and very high. They were Danites, the league of vengeance.

They paraded on Union Square carrying rifles inlaid with nielloed silver. They wore green silk masks and under the holes for the eyes there glistened tears of gold. Their gloves made of antelope hide were embroidered at the cuffs with native gold and tiny shells, their moccasins were covered in multicoloured feathers contrasting with one another in delicate motifs. Behind the Amerindians smoking on the ground stood these magnificent Danites, as the procession of wives criss-crossed the square in all directions. And floating over the noise of the crowd you might have caught the words Exterminators, Angles, Love, Eternity, Music, Death, Vengeance, Kisses, and Slavery.

And then people of all races began to appear. There were Scandinavian men in short trousers and striped stockings of white and blue, all wearing a gold earring. There were Russian men in red smocks, with long hair and green caps which had long visors, and which they wore at an acute angle over their eyes. There were Englishmen displaying chin-strap beards and well-trimmed moustaches, clean-shaven Americans with a rabbit-foot of hair down to their ear-lobes, and a few heavily bearded Jews in long houpelandes. And Germans in cloth caps, many of whom wore glasses. They were all Mormons and all the processions came and stood by the Danites and the squatting Native Americans. An Ute woman was also in amongst them, hideous to look at she was so wrinkled, and the sores on her shoulders, her face and her head were covered in flies sucking the bloody sanies that were oozing from them.

Then there were still more Mormons of every race, some encased in well-cut frock coats and flared collars, all with the same knots in their ties; others dressed poorly but decently.

There was also a blind man who came along lead by two children, barefoot and trembling all over. He was dressed only in trousers and a shirt, and he wore bracelets on his wrists made of rope strung with nuggets of pierced gold. He had a necklace of the same kind and a belt as well. It was he who had discovered gold in California in 1840. They said that he'd been trembling from a fever ever since; and that he'd transmitted this fever to the whole world. It was also said that he'd been blinded by the brilliance of the gold, and that now rich and with many wives he came every day to Union Square to tell his story:

'I was coming home to the Latter-Day Saints from the war in Mexico, crossing California on foot, working here and there and travelling on, taking jobs whenever I ran out of food… One day I was working for a former captain in the Swiss guards of the French King Charles X, thinking of my brothers and my wives, and I saw a nugget as I bent over to wash in the stream from the water-mill. I knew immediately what it was, I'd seen a money-lender with some of them before, in Frisco. I kept my discovery secret for several weeks, and afterwards everything was known but I was rich by then, it's thanks to me that our nation was saved from bankruptcy. I was God's chosen instrument for the completion of Joseph Smith's prophecy, and his prediction that the notes he wrote and had no use for would one day be worth as much as gold. I'm the one who found all the gold for our money, the most precious money there is, cast in pure gold. And now no Mormon is allowed to prospect for gold.'

And the nuggets he wore about his person gave him a wild and untamed air.

In other gatherings Gentiles living in the Mormon city were mingling together. Just like the Mormons there were people of all races, Americans,

Dutch, Italians, Mexicans. There were also Negroes, many Chinese, some Hawaiians and Japanese as well, whole monogamous families of trappers, nomads, desperados from the Mexican border, Catholic missionaries and missionaries from other sects, deserters from various European navies who had jumped ship in California and been attracted by the wealth of the new city. Men and women alike looked at the Mormon gathering and the encampment of newly arrived women with a sort of disdain, and in the middle of this assembly of Gentiles, talking loudly and full of affectation, with mannered gestures, grand airs and an effortlessly noble manner, a troupe of thespians was making its way. There was to be a performance that evening in the theatre, and the actress at the head was so blond, so slim, so majestic. She had a train behind her carried by the director of the troupe, a small hunchback in a black frock coat and a top hat, she would smile at the women and sweep aside with her fan any men in her way. She came to a stop when her comrade actors and actresses dissuaded her with loud cries and long declamations from drifting past the assemblies and into the processions of wives that kept flowing in.

Wives of Elder Lubel Perciman, fourteen in number, all wearing black faille dresses with flame-coloured lace trim. They bore the name of their husband and were told apart by their given names. Wives also of The Lion of the Almighty, the Prophet Brigham Young. He had twenty-four, the youngest was thirteen and two were over thirty, one thirty-eight and the other fifty-four. They were called by their number and wife number 19, who was twenty-four, kept turning back and looking passionately over at the Danites. They were all very elegant and wore valuable jewellery. There was also the troupe of Walter Ruffin's twenty-four wives, The Vine of Canaan. Their grey dresses dragged along in the dust behind them, they wore large black felt hats with a crown like a flattened stove-pipe, with a wide brim that stretched out all round, curving up in front and behind. The eleven wives of The Perfection of the Sun were there, Robin Formesnear. One of them wore red linen, that was my mother, two wore puce silk dresses, two others wore starched skirts of white canvas with pink braces and yellow bodices, four had short skirts, some blue, some green, with big tartan bows of yellow, black and red on their behind, and the last had a shimmering knee-length silk dress. They all had dishevelled hair, and on their heads they wore small Native American tiaras with white and red feathers. They bore the name of their husband preceded by the name of their father. All were pregnant and the pregnancy of each one seemed very advanced. Their enormous bellies swayed out in front of them and gave them a noble look.

Other women were pushing in behind. Like turbulent rivers they flowed down all the streets, and wherever the émigrées looked they would see other women and almost all of them were pregnant. There were so many that the assemblies of Mormons as well as Gentiles were lost in them, and soon there were so many pregnant women that on the whole of Union Square it seemed like there was nothing but their enormous bellies moving about like little waves on a lake, on the surface of which their pregnant and puffy faces would bob up and down like corks.

And the émigrées wondered at so much fecundity after the sterility of the Salt Flats. The religion they had espoused back in Europe is the religion of fecundity. And soon, mingling with the women from afar these fecund matrons were praising their happiness, describing the joys of their home life, and lauding the strength and the intelligence of their husbands.

'Come with me, young woman, there's already four of us and we live together with our husband. Come and share our common tenderness. Our children are still young, they will never know which one of us is there mother, and their filial piety will include all five of us.'

'Come with me, oh young woman, five wives live at home and our husband has another three, two were alive in times past and the other will be born three centuries from now.'

'Come with me, oh young woman, you will be fecund in our nation of fecundity. It will cover the world and then will be the time of greatest felicity.'

'Come with me, oh young woman, my husband has fifteen wives, you will be the most cherished because you are the most beautiful.'

'Come with me, oh young woman. There are twenty of us wives and we each have our own home in an orchard full of fruit and our husband visits us in turn.'

'Come with me, oh young woman, I came from Europe as well one day. I'd lost my one true love, and this is the city without love. What happiness can compare to the satisfactions of the flesh and a mind that knows no jealousy?'

And the pregnant wives all wanted to seduce the European women and bring them to their husband. They spoke enthusiastically about happiness without love and without jealousy. And almost every one had forgotten their words of affection from the past.

Their bellies prophesied the greatness of their nation to come. Their descendants would proliferate all over the world.

In each home several wives would encourage each other, help each other and look after each other, and arrange things so that the husband, freed from the anxieties of the flesh by the variety of its satisfactions, could devote himself to wealth-making endeavours; and as the needs of the household grew, the fecundity of the wives would increase the activity of the man.

There were now three assemblies gathered on Union Square: the assembly of Gentiles where inferior men had also gathered, black men, yellow men, and the whole feral population of fortune-seekers; the assembly of Mormons, accompanied by the Lamanites, who had lost the memory of Christ's teachings on American soil, after the Resurrection; and finally the assembly of wives, where Mormon womanhood was displaying its pomp and promise for the future to the women of Europe.

Suddenly the whole square was in turmoil, all eyes turned to towards the wide avenue where a small troupe of men was majestically making its way. They were dressed in black and wore top hats. It was the Council of Twelve: Weber C. Kimball, The Herald of Grace; Perley P. Pratt, The Archer of Heaven; Orson Hyde, The Olive Branch of Israel; Willard Richards, Keeper of the Archives; William Smith, The Staff of Jacob; Wilfred Woodruff, The Banner of the Gospel; George A. Smith, The Entablature of Truth; Orson Pratt, The Gauge of Philosophy; John Page, The Sundial; Liman Wight, The Wild Ram of the Mountains. John Taylor, Champion of the Righteous, was travelling in Europe and absent. And bringing up the rear The Lion of the Almighty, Brigham Young himself, likened to St Peter. He was the second prophet of Mormonism, founder of the new nation, and President of the Latter-Day Saints. He was talking quietly with Lorenzo Snow, the Elder who had accompanied the neophytes on their journey from Europe.

Seeing these illustrious figures the Mormon wives gathered into their troupes, and leaving the émigrées where they were, went over to join the ranks of the Saints. Lorenzo Snow presented the newly arrived sisters to the Prophet and the men who'd travelled with them came over from the Gentiles where they'd been mingling, and were presented as well. Several unions were concluded between émigrées and Mormons who asked their hand, as well as one between two émigrées and a European man from the wagon-train. The Prophet himself augmented his harem with a Norwegian woman who couldn't stop blushing, a spirited English one in Mexican clothes appealingly moulded to her form, and a Hungarian who'd not learnt a word of English during the voyage, whereas her companions from Norway, Germany, Denmark, Italy and Switzerland had all got on with it, even the only French woman who'd been persuaded to come.

These new arrivals were married now, only the French woman dressed like a sailor was left. She'd refused the proposal of every Mormon, the Prophet himself had asked her to enter his harem, he'd been rebuffed like all the others. Brigham Young looked at her closely for a moment, then invited her to his home until whenever she would decide to marry. The emigrants, both men and women all joined the assembly of Mormons: the existing wives joyously welcomed their new sisters, the members of the Council of Twelve went and stood by their wives, and now there were only two assemblies, Mormons and Gentiles, with Brigham Young in front of both and the capricious French woman crouching close by. She was missing her three dark rooms full of knickknacks and frills on a street up a hill in Paris, the quadrilles at The Grand Charterhouse where

she'd made her debut in a liberty cap, under an immense tent which was called a Moroccan tent because of Bugeaud's victory at the Battle of Isly. Distant regrets… She'd danced opposite a worker *à la mode*. Distant regrets. She'd been a grisette amongst soldiers in their embroidered finery, and bohemian students, and appies in splattered overalls. Distant regrets.

In Bréda she was known as Lorette and would hum:

> Lorette the brunette
> Would quietly coo
> Love good Sir
> And less of the chew!

But on Union Square Brigham Young had raised his arms: Mormons and Gentiles alike, all men removed their hats. And the Prophet began to speak. He lauded the nobility of the new religion, its openness to all truth as it is revealed. He rejoiced in the Angels that the Gods had sent amongst the sacred nation. He enjoined the wealthy to distribute their surplus to the poor. He exalted polygamy and the work of the flesh.

'It is the immense joy of man to be able to procreate in the image of divinity. And some would have us limit the creative power of man to the womb of a single woman? Is that not to insult the power of generation? And does the creative power of man cease with the pregnancy of his wife? Why prohibit man from procreation in times of pregnancy? Be fruitful and multiply, children of the Gods! Voluptuousness makes us divine, and when we know it, we rise to Heaven. Be born, be welcomed into the world, sons and daughters of the Saints; be fruitful and multiply in the name of Merer, Odiroth, Merevos, Marinikambinissim….'

And he continued speaking in revelations. The emotion of the whole crowd of Mormons and Gentiles grew to fever pitch, and the eyes of everyone shone like igneous rock. Then piercing cries came from the crowd as the Prophet spoke. Arms began to wave in the air, and the pregnant women laughed so loudly they couldn't support the weight of their bellies and fell to the ground. There were extravagant cries from everywhere, the Native Americans made guttural sounds like a knell ringing, then there were shrieks from Gentile women, and some of the men began to tremble and weep with fear. The raucous cries of the Mormon women turned to screaming and wailing, and a number of people fainted with a piercing cry like the sinister call of a bird of ill-omen. And then the whole crowd was rocked by a crazy frenzy, everyone was shaken with crazy barking, and everyone who hadn't fainted was on all fours barking like mad dogs, with their heads turned to Brigham Young. The sermon continued, the voice of the Prophet speaking in revelations trumpeted above the howling of the men and the women. He was shouting with all his might, his eyes turned to the heavens with his top hat on the back of his head. His neck was distended from the effort, the button on his flared collar had cracked, his tie was climbing up his neck, his shirt was open and the Prophet's goitre stretched down over his stomach like the udder of a cow. He thundered on, and lent down to look into the eyes of all the people barking and crawling up to him on all fours, grunting and showing their teeth.

Then he took off his frock coat and waved it above his head shouting inarticulate sounds. All the dogs of madness stood up and suddenly Union Square was still, and the Prophet continued in revelations.

Soon the crowd was seized with frenzied convulsions: pregnant women had violent spasms as if about to give birth; men went into contortions like rope, and a troupe of women ran backwards around the square with their heads had turned back to front. The Native Americans' eyes hung out from their sockets and stuck to their faces like spiders on a web. It was convulsions and jerks everywhere, every face was transformed and unrecognisable, and physiognomies changed from one second to the next.

Then as the fervour was intensified still more by the cries of the Prophet, everyone crouched like frogs and began to leap about waving their arms, or went into grotesque and gruesome contortions like unimaginable reptiles. The voice of the Prophet began to soften, now he spoke soothingly and the contortions fell away. Everyone threw themselves to the ground and began to roll from side to side like a child being rocked. But their movements accelerated and some rolled rigidly all around Union Square and back, over each other, bashing into each other, hurting each other.

And still waving his coat Brigham Young began to chant, his shrill and shrieking modulations shook the bodies of everyone in the crowd, they all stood up at once and bent backwards into a circle, and with their heads touching their heels in imperfect hoops they began to rotate all over the Square.

They rolled everywhere by the thousand, as the Prophet sang on in the declining sun. Using his coat as a whip he scourged these human hoops and chased them into all the adjoining streets, and there they unfolded and came to a stop with a terrifying cry, covered in dust and blood-stained drool."

Chapter Five

"It's frightening," said Elvira after a few moments, as old man Warning was calming down a little. "It's really frightening. There was I thinking it would be such fun to be a Mormon."

"Polygamy doesn't sound like a sinecure, from what I'm hearing," observed the pseudo-Ovid, whose bravura was demonstrated by the palm leaf and the two stars he was wearing, one of silver the other of gold. "And becoming a fanatic is as dangerous as attacking a trench mounted with a machine-gun."

"These scenes of fanaticism, extremely common in America some thirty years before, were extremely rare at the time I'm talking about.

But let me continue.

One evening at dinner time the wealthy Elder Lubel Perciman came home with a new wife to whom he had just been sealed in marriage by the Prophet. It was the French woman Pamela Monsenergues, who from then on would be known as Pamela Perciman.

For a long time she had resisted advances from all the young Mormon women, married and unmarried alike, and when she finally decided in favour of Lubel Perciman, it was because his wives were young and pleasing to look at, and because they had visited the French woman Pamela in the home of Brigham Young where she had been the recipient of his hospitality."

"That's my grandmother alright," said Elvira, "She liked women, and I've never met a woman either whom I've not found appealing."

Elvira's remark drew no response from Ovid, and Warning proceeded with his story.

"Lubel Perciman had fourteen wives and each one was young and graceful. They were like a flower-bed grown in different climates. Five were English, two were from Illinois, one from Pennsylvania and another from Massachusetts, there were two Danes, an Irish woman and a Dutch one, a Russian and a German.

Pamela had not agreed without conditions to sealing her marriage to the Elder, who in a few years had amassed a Mormon fortune by looking after the businesses of Brigham Young, a man of great financial understanding who'd had the original idea of establishing huge shops like you see in all the great cities, and where you can buy everything.

Pamela had insisted that the marriage would only be sealed when she had a white dress to wear, and with the help of the wives of the Prophet she cut it and sewed herself to her own pattern. She hadn't dared ask for orange blossom, believing she no longer had the right; but on the day of the ceremony she chose a crown of white roses, and wore the necklace her fiancé had given her made of enormous pearls like union pearls, so called after the Jugurthine War.

During the sealing ceremony she was deathly sad, in her heart she was full of nostalgia and anxiety. And in her mind, she compared herself to the rivers of California and Utah that she had seen during her voyage, with thousands of snakes teaming at the bottom. She felt a thousand different sadnesses, and the strange ceremonies left her cold and increased her pain.

A carriage was to take the newly-weds to their lodging, and it so happened that at the very moment Lubel Perciman was helping Pamela onto the footboard, a rider passed close by at the walk on a black mare. He was dressed in a long white robe and on the mask covering his face she recognised the green wolf and the golden tears of the Danites. His tiara, high and immaculate, gave him an imposing air. And Pamela's heart began to beat faster: 'There's the man I should have married. He's mysterious and he's handsome, and instead my businessman Lubel looks like nothing but a parvenu, with his chin-strap beard.' Thoughts of adultery and escape began to cross her mind, she wished the Danite would take her on the back of his horse and ride into another country, then she shuddered as she remembered the terrible reputation of the Danites, and she clung to her husband who hardly looked at her and said not a word. When she arrived in her new house and saw the fourteen wives waiting to greet her, and the way they were standing in rows in the middle of the room, she burst out laughing and thought: 'My conjugal home is distinctly odd! All you need is a black woman and you'd have a full house!' Then she was sad, and said to her husband she should like to collect her thoughts, to get used to this new and strange life, and she spent the night alone."

"The fact is," said Elvira, as Mr Warning was enjoying a pinch of snuff, "the fact is, this is all quite out of the ordinary. I saw some very peculiar things in Russia, and George, my first lover, showed me all sorts, but I've never seen a harem. That must be quite unusual! Perhaps living in a harem might not be too bothersome after all for those like me who find women very agreeable."

"After the war you may yet experience it," said the pseudo-Ovid St Euxine. "But now I think of it, and granting my great-uncle's account poses the problem correctly, the response of European institutions and attitudes would certainly be negative."

"O people of a land where nothing changes," pronounced Otto Warning sententiously, "let any man in Europe who is not polygamous cast the first stone on the Mormons!"

And after another pinch he resumed his narrative.

"The following morning, with the sound of parchment being shuffled like the rattle on a snake, the fifteen wives of the Elder Perciman, in low-cut ruffled dresses made of moire, came out of their garden and paused for a moment on the corner, close by the house of Orson Spencer, on the north-western side of the junction where Council House Street intersects with Emigration Street.

The four Americans could easily be distinguished from the others, they had enormous, beautiful hair mixed with extraordinary quantities of false hair, and their face, neck, bust and arms were covered with immoderate amounts of starch powder. The five English wives wore their hair of rose gold in royal diadems, and its colours of the sunrise made them look like burning candles, perfectly white.

The two Danish wives, the Russian one and the Dutch one had their heavy plaits wound into thick buns at the back, while the black hair falling in loose coils of the Irish wife emphasized the spirited pallor of her face. Only the French woman Pamela had chestnut hair like an otter's fur.

And so they went, all fifteen of them, along the streets of the New City. The shops were all closed, for that day in 1852 was the 29th September, a day of great celebration, the day the Prophet Brigham Young proclaimed to the people the revelation of polygamy. Doors were closed to the public, but in the windows there were meticulous displays in quite barbarous decorative taste.

The photographer Mersenne Cannon was showing daguerreotypes of the principle Mormon figures and their wives.

William Henefer, barber and restaurateur, with bottles of American wine from Catawba County and Isabella County, also Champagne bottles and Port bottles, and bars of soap in white, pink and green, bottles of Cologne as well and tins of food, had assembled a bizarre edifice representing the Temple the Mormons built in Nauvoo, Illinois. William Nixon had huge piles of potatoes and grain, wheat as well as corn, also melons, to the astonishment of everyone in the middle of this arid desert.

John and Enoch Reese, general store, had pyramids of tinned oysters and jars of jam, and in between them there were suede clothes, ropes, arms and ammunition, sacks of coffee, barrels of salt pork and flour. There were shops with signs such as *Fashions of Paris and Deseret*. In Main Street there were bookshops, there were dairies, there was The Grand Utah Hotel owned by an Italian from Piedmont who was also a dentist, a grocer and a trader. He had tied all his mules to the fence in front of his establishment, they stood there quietly, precious beasts to anyone travelling across mountains and deserts, some black with clear expressive eyes and high as a mare, others small, lively and gracious, and reminding you easily of very large mice. These mules had little beehives over their ears, which are a symbol of Mormonism, and every time a horse passed by in the street or a street nearby, they would pull at their tether and try to follow. There were too many for them all to be lined in front of the hotel, and the row stretched as far the shops of James Needham, George P. Bourne, and John Chillett the furrier, who was whittling a piece of wood as he talked on the stoop with a hunter telling him about the parts of the country where he'd been, Tennessee, Arkansas, and The Red River. And everywhere, on the shops, on the houses, on the Museum, on the Tabernacle, on Endowment House, on Lion House with its portico, everywhere the symbol of the beehive, carved or painted, or otherwise the revered name of Deseret, and everywhere "the all-seeing eye" surrounded by sunrays, the sacred emblem of the Latter-Day Saints.

And so the fifteen wives of the Elder Lubel Perciman made their way to the Tabernacle of Mormon Theocracy where the ceremony had just ended, and where the Prophet had proclaimed the dogma of polygamy to the Latter-Day Saints and the entire universe. To add still more majesty to this consecration of virile power, a ritual procession was leaving the Tabernacle and making its way around the city.

At the head of the procession, carrying the trowel and the carpenter's square, were the pontiffs who had raised the first buttresses on the banks of the American promised land, and behind them carrying the same emblems came the sculptors, the architects and the masons who were building the temple.

Then, pulled along by bullocks driven by five young squaws draped in a cloak with a yellow trim, with long lashes and straight shiny black hair that partially hid their faces, and decorated with strings of claws, turquoise stones, sea shells, clay pendants and a medicine sac embroidered with pearls, came a float carrying an enormous cage with thirteen eagles, one for each of the original States, they flapped their wings to sounds sung in their own language and the exquisite tones of the Native American women.

Behind the float came the trumpet blasts of the militia marching behind the standard bearer, and it was followed by a troupe of musicians dressed in American costumes with wide-brimmed pointed hats, playing fifes, clarinets and oboes. Their music alternated with the music of the trumpets and the other brass instruments in the band of Ballo the Sicilian and the singers who followed, dressed as pioneers and carrying Native American bags.

Then came a detachment of the Mormon militia marching in good order and commanded by Captain Pettigrew. In the middle there were four black slaves carrying a large hive symbolizing the territory of Utah, and calling to mind the name of Deseret revealed to the Prophet, the land of the little bee.

At that moment a Negro from the banks of the Missouri jostled against the fifteen wives of Elder Lubel Perciman. He had arrived that very morning pushing his wheel-barrow, travelling with a trapper from Michigan fresh from setting his traps along the River Jordan and the shores of Lake Utah. He wore a blue shirt and had a tranquil eye, and he was trumpeting his goods all around the city, stopping every now and again to dance a gigue in front of the houses that looked the most opulent, and that was when he pushed these women in evening gowns roughly out of the way. Standing aside, the American ones cried out irately and recovering quickly from their initial fear, fell upon the unwelcome creature and rained blows upon him with their fans. He wanted to speak to the Prophet who was taking his place in the procession near the Patriarch, together with the Apostles, but instead he tripped and fell to the ground in front of this august parade.

The President stopped and the whole line came to a halt behind him, and as the trumpets continued to sound the Negro cried out:

'I have seen Christ-Adam coming down with his wives from the orange sky, and gods stretching over the infinity of space were gathered to proclaim the Redemption of the Blacks.'

But Brigham Young turned to Kimball who was laughing rudely and enquired:

'What evil spirit is trapped for his sins in the tabernacle of this lying nigger?'

And four men emerged from the company of the Septuagint coming up behind, and without permission took the scarf the French woman Pamela was wearing on her arm, twisted the long silk ribbon into a rope, tied it in a slipknot and threw it over a strong branch in the mulberry tree by the side of the road. And seizing the Negro who began to struggle and was desperately crying

'I am Sam Candland, son of the State of Missouri',
and
'I'm a Yankee!',
they hung him to the applause of everyone watching, and laughter cascaded from the American women whose eyes shone from the pleasure at being so promptly avenged.

The hanged man was still struggling, his feet danced the gigue with all the agility he had taught them, and on his black face his eyes seemed like two big scorpions marching against each other. The general joy reached its height when a stream of saliva came out of his mouth and a musician in the Nauvoo orchestra, a one-time whaler, cried 'There she blows!', just like a sailor scouring the sea from the mast-top.

With the last convulsions of the Negro from Missouri the procession went on its way, leaving the dead man's fixed stare behind them, and his body as rigid as an opium-eater's.

At the very front a huge model of a seated woman was processing, she wore a crown of stars and there were two men pushing her along on wheels concealed inside the plinth. A third turned her head from side to side to make her look like a living woman, and when from time to time this prodigious replica would speak, it was these same men shouting from inside the machine.

'I am American Democracy from the land of big women and turbulent men who together make giants more enormous than the enormous sequoias.'

Then there was the council of the bishops and the colleges of lesser-order priests, followed by a few Ute medicine men walking behind the float of The Scriptures and the Press, on which were piled the papyruses of Abraham, translations in manuscript of the Book of Mormon by Joseph Smith, and the first books and newspapers printed by the Mormons. It was surrounded by the family of Joseph Smith who together led the bullocks that pulled it. On top the patriarch, a young man standing with his eyes closed, was holding a silver casket containing Urim and Thummim, the divine instruments of revelation.

There was a crowd of virgins dressed in white muslin and wearing the colours of all the nations of the world, and Mr Phelps followed about ten yards behind with his eyes down. People were terrified at the sight of him, because rumour had it he represented the devil at the endowment ceremonies where dowries were agreed. Behind came a long line of children carrying placards with Mormon writing, sometimes their singing sounded like the ga-ga's of geese, and sometimes with a crescendo like a trumpet their young voices reminded us of the howl of a swan from the North.

Then before the crowd of the faithful, Mormon dignitaries began to process in tight rows, talking amongst themselves as they went. Lubel Perciman stepped away to greet his wives with whom he was to dine later at Kimball's house, where there would be an entertainment and afterwards dancing. He went up to Pamela, asked her if she thought she could grow accustomed to Mormon life, and added:

'You know full well, Pamela, that my desires are as yet unfulfilled. I have married you, but have not exercised my rights as a husband. I have respected the scruples I imagine you might still have, and did not force myself on you yesterday when the time came. I was waiting for today's festival and for the Prophet to proclaim the Revelation of polygamy. Marrying many wives is now part of our dogma and this evening I shall be united with you in all sanctity.'

But Pamela was hardly listening. The Danites were passing by at that moment, their horses at the walk and resplendent in white, and she could barely tear her eyes from the one at the front whose masked face turned towards her for a moment. In the crowd watching the parade there were also a few federal officers who would smile whenever they their eyes crossed with any of the Mormon women's, and Pamela saw that one of them was always looking over his shoulder to where the Prophet's wives were standing. Wife 19 often looked across at him and together their eyes were the colour of wet myrtle. There was a group of people separating them and a Jew called Chéri de Mendoza was standing there, he had bowed his head as the float went by with the papyruses written in the very hand of Abraham, displayed with so much pomp. After which he had gone back to the conversation he was having with Chief Milopitz of the Ute people, who spoke to him in short bursts in a guttural-sounding English without any 'f's, because of the difficulty this people has with pronouncing that consonant. The Ute had walked up to Chéri de Mendoza and called him 'brother', and the Jew who had never met him asked why.

'Don't you know,' the Indian had replied, 'that according to the Mormon witness we are descendants of the same race?'

Chéri de Mendoza thought about it as he bowed his head to the relics of Abraham as they passed.

'I believe you,' he said raising his head again. 'There are certainly analogies between the customs and rituals of our two nations. The word Ute is pronounced more or less like the German word for Jew, which could well be a sign of its Judaic origin. But really our spirits are hardly alike. Even though the spirit of race and family, the spirit of tradition as a whole inspires us both, the misfortunes which have struck us Jews, and our position in relation to all other races so very different from ours, have given us a real ability to understand innovation and make use of it. We have a practical mind not only for material things, but everything to do with intelligence and the soul. But you on the other hand, even though you're attached to your traditions you don't preserve them or keep them pure, in other words living and modern. You belong to the ten plebeian tribes, and we belong to the royal tribe of Judah. That difference between us explains the lowly state in which we find you now, it also explains our genius, which is to dominate by buying assets and with our judeifying rituals, look at how the judeification of the whole Mediterranean basin is fast becoming a reality. And by the way, Mr Ute Chief, don't forget that I've opened a curiosity shop on Main Street, I'll give you a good price for anything you may wish to sell, any curiosity or archaeological object like weapons, cloth, leather goods, artefacts with feathers, engraved stonework, sculptures and pottery. I'll find homes for them all in the private collections of the East as well as the museums of Europe.'

And the whole being of Chéri de Mendoza, a fine example himself of the judeification he was heralding, was living proof that Negro and Chinese blood flows in the blood of the Israelites.

The Ute Chief Milopitz looked gravely and not without contempt at this man, very possibly of his own race, proposing to sell the evidence of its glorious history. He shook his head and turned to his wife standing humbly by, bent under the weight of the heavy bundle on her back. In each of the two men lived ignorance, superstition, stupidity and salaciousness, something more base than the plebs; but unaware as they were, the beliefs and practices of the State were being modelled upon them. For just as man is made from the salt of the earth, nations grow from the plebs."

Chapter Six

"I must admit I have great admiration for my grandmother. She was able to refuse men, whereas today, although women have more rights than in earlier times, it is much more difficult for them to refuse male advances, even when like me, and my grandmother as well from what I can guess, they are generally drawn to women, and vulnerable to very few crushes on a very small number of men. This evening I want to draw the portrait of a Danite. The one you're telling us about reminds me strangely of Pablo Goldentail."

"Gracious me, I don't think I ever saw a Danite without his green mask," said Mr Warning. "But it's getting late and I have let myself get carried away by my reminiscences. I must try and abridge the rest of my account.

The long table had been set in the auditorium of Social Hall, the theatre of Salt Lake City. Kimball was there hosting the celebration, surrounded by his wives, Brigham Young was there too and his entire family, also Lubel Perciman and his harem, and other Mormons with their wives. Families had not been grouped together, instead men and women were seated alternately and Pamela was between Chéri de Mendoza and James Ferguson, an officer in the Utah Militia who was also a lawyer, an orator and an actor. He was about thirty years old, strong, energetic and witty; his social graces made him sought after for all the celebrations. Although he was a bachelor he had the reputation of an adulterer, and while recognising his qualities the Mormons also feared him. In front of Pamela there was a federal officer with wife 19 on his left, and on his right the blond actress on tour in Salt Lake City.

Blacks were serving, there were candle-sticks on the table, and in vases made from the local ceramics there were strangely shaped wax flowers, one of the crafts at which the Mormons excelled.

As a first course there were locusts, wild hyacinth root, onions which are the food of Amerindian tribes, and Catawba wine from the vines on the shores of the Ohio.

People listened attentively to Chéri de Mendoza praising the flavour of the roast locusts.

'It's an ancient food,' he was saying, 'but still new to the Europeans and it repels more than a few Whites, even those who claim to be without prejudice. Far from harming custom and healthy tradition, novelty enriches them, it enlivens and fertilizes them. In the same way the wise polygamists of Utah, far from harming the institution of the family, are instead extending its grandeur and its strength.'

Brigham Young, hearing these words, turned to him and said:

'Mormons are a chosen people, walking this earth within an anointed spiritual sphere, taking account neither of human laws nor the superficial riches of the world.'

And pouring himself some more Catawba, the Prophet raised his glass to Chéri de Mendoza who first of all drank to the health of the ladies and then to the Prophet's.

The Blacks were hurrying to change the table, salmon trout from Lake Utah was served and the curtain went up on the stage at the end of the hall.

The décor consisted of a wall-hanging with the All-Seeing-Eye in the middle, a young woman representing America and a young man representing Europe met in front of it, one entering from the side of the yard, the other from the side of the garden. A dialogue ensued which I can remember almost in its entirety because the following year we had to learn it by heart in school.

Europe

Nations, I offer you order and beauty
Ruins with the grace of young women
Rivers like the lines of great poets
And all my slavery and all my royalty
All my enchanted gods which are my faith and my art
All my quarrelsome peoples and the fragrant flowers
You Churches where your ancestors and believers came to kneel
Oh you aged houses where progress was weaned
Crossroads where epochs chose a path and went on their way

And fatherlands and homelands and motherlands in whose flags I
    am dressed
Phantoms oh forests of genius where each tree is a human name
Oh forest walking backwards without ever walking away
I am all the phantoms and all the shadows
The homelands the cities the fields of battle
America oh my daughter and the daughter of Columbus.

America

Men who suffer oh women who love and you children too
Come and draw the waters of your second baptism
From the blue lake where the Mississippi draws its flow
I am the wide spaces of hope and the future without memory
Among the herds of wild horses out of the horses of Europe
Roam flocks of young thoughts from the thoughts of Europe
And new truths are revealed to those tired of the old
They sing or cry or pray or guffaw
And turn our minds to new creations
A new god rises from a boat made of bark
A goddess combs her hair and sings in the prairies of wild rice
Still other gods demand still other heroes
And now there's a ship
Listen to the Quadroon Ball and the sound of shifty voyagers dancing
And hear the lament from far over the horizon
The lament of dying Europeans remembering
The prairies of wild rice on the shores of the Mississippi
And the copses of black cypresses draped in silvery tillandsia!

Europe and America joined hands and sang in unison:

The sea separates the two spouses
But now it's the wedding of two enormous continents
From one a ship bursts across the ocean
Europe fertilizes America
The virile name of Europe in the language of diplomacy
The international language that is French
The masculine is clearly heard
And the feminine in French the language of Nations

Clearly marks the sex of America
Europe frenetically extends the rigid Armor peninsula
And America spreads wide and open
Where the isthmus trembles at the tropics
A sublime love between nations is born from the wild couple
With elements made for marriage
The ship continues its fertilising voyage
The wind swells its moaning sails
And cries the voluptuous cry of giants in love.

At that moment little boys dressed as Native Americans and little girls dressed as old ladies came and danced around Europe and America, who kissed and embraced to the loud applause of all the guests. After which a few theatre-lovers were allowed in for the performance of *Jedediah the Great*. They had paid for their tickets in kind, melons, and pottery, etc.

Chinamen came and removed the tables while Blacks began to play music, which prompted Mormon-style dancing – two women for every man. Chairs and benches were put in position and soon the stage lit up, the lights in the auditorium were put out, and as people danced on waiting for the curtain to rise suddenly the doors opened and federal officers entered the hall. Soldiers lit the way with burning torches.

The dancing stopped and Kimball went up the new arrivals to protest at their intrusion, but five officers rushed up to the Mormon wives, seized them bodily and dragged them away before the Mormons could think of preventing them. The federal officer who had been at the dinner, and who was dancing with Pamela and wife 19, pushed them towards his brothers-in-arms. They were outside before Militia Officer Ferguson, who had a small part in *Jedidiah the Great* and was putting on his make-up, was able to chase after them with the Danites.

The abductors had horses at the ready, they hoisted their precious cargo onto them and galloped from the city.

It was a frenetic ride and more dead than alive Pamela was resigned to anything. After half an hour she thought other horses were riding up behind them. The abductors rode all the harder, but the others were in hot pursuit and gaining ground. Soon there was gunfire and the horse carrying Pamela collapsed under her, and when she recovered from her faint all she saw was the mask of a Danite contemplating her with his tears of gold.

'Thank you for saving me,' she said to him.

'I'm sorry I could save only you,' he replied, 'The others have all been kidnapped by the Gentiles.'

And Pamela recalled Wife 19 and thought:

'She's escaped, that's what she wanted.'

At that moment other Danites arrived with a mule for Pamela and she came back to Salt Lake City, riding her mule and led by the dazzling Danite who had captured her from her abductors.

Lubel Perciman was there to greet her and celebrate her return, but Brigham Young made no appearance that day nor the following week, his favourite wife had taken flight for good.

As the night grew silent and the moon glowed with a light both bright and cold, Elder Lubel Perciman, carefully shaven, dressed in blue canvas trousers and moccasins with versicoloured glass beads, and wishing to know the full extent of his conjugal bliss, came into Pamela's bedroom. The smile on his face came from knowing the Danites were outside watching over the wellbeing of the Mormons. The pale stars carried the gods of omnipotence to infinity, and beyond these gods, still other gods more powerful still filled the plenitude of the world with an energy as yet uncreated, and knowing no end.

First Elder Lubel Perciman held up the burning torch he was carrying to look at his image in the mirror. His hair was nicely arranged, he thought, his thin face looked handsome, and his yellow hair was like a luminous hearth nourishing the moon of the American night. Only then did he glance at the bed where your grandmother would be sleeping, like a goddess wrecked by exile and fatigue. But the torch nearly fell from the hand of Elder Lubel Perciman, for the bed was empty. Pamela had no sooner arrived than fled, and my story must end here for your grandmother was never seen nor heard of again among the Mormons, nor was the Danite either as it happens. It was assumed they had run away together, but silence reigned on the subject because people feared the anger of Elder Lubel Perciman, who never spoke another word about her. For myself I heard nothing more at all until this wretched nephew of mine came with a message from you, and reminded me of this pretty and mutinous young woman with wild hair, who made such an impression on the Latter-Day Saints when she arrived on Union Square dressed as a sailor. I forgot to say that the rumour gradually spread that the Danite who disappeared on the same day was none other than the Angel Moroni."

"An Angel!" cried Elvira. "Well, as the granddaughter of the woman whose story you've just told, I certainly feel wings growing out of my shoulders, but I shall be doing my best to keep a grip on them because I've every intention of staying a woman, and have no inclination for aviation at all."

"Your grandmother lacked neither good sense nor honesty," put in the fantasy Ovid, "since she came back to her country to marry and start her family line. Doesn't that say everything we need to know about the moral value of legalised polygamy? The French are just as likely to become Mormon as Turkish. But we'll repopulate the country all the same, don't you worry! It's first and foremost a question of propaganda."

Chapter Seven

Wounded during a patrol and taken away by ambulance to an auxiliary hospital, and from there to Val-de-Grâce, from his very first outings Anatole Holybest found that Paris no longer astonished him as it had on his first furlough. He met Coralie whom he had known from a distance before the war, because from December 1913 she had been the partner of a friend of his, Hyacinth Brionne, just then killed at the front. They became intimate, and she never left his side as he convalesced and began in a certain way to resume his life from before the war, meeting young writers and avant-garde artists.

Every religious feeling in Anatole Holybest had been transported onto the field of social honour. He loved his county above all else, or rather he loved the collectivity that he wished for France and that France constituted in his mind: jealous of its traditions, but also highly audacious in the pursuit of progress.

"Which is why," he was saying one day, "the sight of ruins can move me in exactly the same way as a pregnant woman, I feel I can see what will emerge from them both. And however affected I am, to me those who have died invoke the future repopulation of France. In the next fifty years she must become a country of a hundred million inhabitants."

"Establish Mormonism," replied the imaginary Ovid, "and let every man have children with several women."

In the same moment Pablo Canouris, also known as Pablo Dogsdick, was saying quietly to Elvira:

"Since Nicolas has gone and you're my mistress there's no reason to stay at his. Come and live with me."

But Elvira's eyes were sparkling in the dark, and as she held Pablo Canouris's arm she was thinking about Mavis waiting for her at home, about caresses of indefinite sweetness, not caresses she might receive but caresses she would give and which touch only the heart of a woman. They had all been on an excursion to the studios of Montmartre, and as night fell they were walking home, singing as they went:

> Fat'ma
> Lived in the Kasbah
> In deepest Algeriah
> Not prett-ee ee-ee
> But still all the sidi's
> Envied ah

After which they all separated in Montparnasse, a Jack for every Jill and a lid for every pot, and on the way Anatole asked Coralie:

"You weren't ever unfaithful to Hyacinth when he was alive?"

"Oh yes," she replied.

"Did he know?" asked Anatole, in indescribable pain.

"He guessed, he told me so in his letters, he was very upset about it," said Coralie.

"Who with?" asked Anatole, his eyes filling to the brim with tears.

"A Jewish man," Coralie replied, "attached to the N-th artillery, but he'd arranged never to be sent to the front. He didn't even sleep in the Nanterre barracks, he'd rented a little villa and stayed there instead.

For the first eight months of the war I was never unfaithful to Hyacinth. I had a friend called Genevieve, I often went out with her and we often went to Nanterre to see her boyfriend. René saw me and followed us right onto the train back to Paris. He made us laugh so much we just had to keep talking. It all happened very fast. I didn't love him but he was so amusing and I was so lonely. One day later when we were arguing I twisted his hand so hard that I broke his little finger. He managed to convince them he'd broken it on duty and got himself reclassified.

When Hyacinth came back on furlough he'd already guessed something, as many of the letters I sent him were postmarked Nanterre. I told him everything. He didn't have the heart to blame me, but I felt how desperate he was and I knew straightaway he would be killed. So then I hated my Jewish man and wanted to die."

Anatole Holybest made no reply, but suddenly he saw the heroic and desperate death of poor Hyacinth Brionne, stretcher-bearer at Bois des Buttes in the Battle of the Aisnes, near Ville-au-Bois in Pontavert.

As the French mounted their assault the lovely forest filled with the sounds from another time of swords, lances and shields. Soldiers advanced silently and stood amongst the trees.

Anatole could imagine the warlike scene and saw in his mind the Ennead at Heliopolis who know all valour. Like the sacred bees flying between the living and the dead, they are the hive of battles immemorial. But lest we forget, our own Nine Worthies comprise both victors and vanquished.

A mirage of Judea began to spread before him, mountains, torrents, a block of green jasper, a bush of thorns here and there, and the trunks of tress cut down. The first of the Nine appeared preceded by a fanfare of horns, it was Joshua crying:

"It's not enough to feed the people. They must be given their promised land of miraculous vines and fountains of milk. Smashing the golden calf isn't everything, the stuff of ditties and dancing. We need ignorance of the laws of nature, we need to stop the golden the sun in the sky and win it. We do not need the happiness of all men, we need for all men to have what is promised them. They hope for victories and the destruction of all other peoples. My hand raised at the sun is the most beautiful monument to the ignorance of humanity, its power, the superhuman power of humanity. By my memory! The sun stopped in its passage, its heat was extinguished, and pining for the sun the enemy took flight in the darkening day."

In the same Judean setting David, the second of the Nine, sang his lament:

"Battles you say? I'm obliged. But alas and alack, no one will be waiting for your return. Those that leave will be forgotten, their people will not miss them and their wives will not remember. Single combat is best! No departures, no long marches of the lost, no returns. Every war is a sin of love. What have been my achievements? An adulterous a war for Bathsheba, who washed her feet in a pond below my terraces in the garden of cedars and cypresses. Women love neither war nor warriors, but gardens of cedars and cypresses, palaces with terraces, and kings who prevaricate. Aged kings who stay home from war, remember Moses who fashioned the ring of oblivion to dampen the indecent feelings that Thaiba harboured for him. And powerful kings, bearded kings going off to war, remember the ring of remembrance Moses made for Sephora his wife when he left for the court of the Pharaoh."

And in the same Judean setting, surrounded by the dead and the dying and crushed by the elephant, Judas Maccabeus, the third of the Worthies, spoke through the rattle of his agony:

"The enemies of your people are like beasts. They must be killed and fought to the death. Kill the beast before the man, yes, but die under the beast if afterwards it will die. No slaughter is enough to repay the dying of a single man. To you the virtuous I say, take animals every day to the altars for sacrifice. And to you the fearless, I say overcome revulsion every day, be butchers for the priests, as they read the entrails on the altars of a great people, raised to its one true God."

A mirage of Anatolia and the swamps of the Troas, the rivers of Simois and Scamander joining at Troy: a hero covered in blood, Hector, the fourth of the Worthies, was speaking.

"Peoples, I call on you to defend yourselves. Trust only women of your own kind, safeguard your gods, your true gods, put no faith in graven images of salvation. And if you can fight a ten-year war, the day will come when as heroes you will die a hero's death. For peoples as well as for men, and for all their gods and all their true gods, the day will come when each will hear the song of the female halcyon so close to me now, the song of death as she comes dancing and battling, often a woman, sometimes a man, and nothing will help, neither valour nor invulnerability. We fall, man and people, on the field of battle, and woe to the survivors, the men and the peoples enslaved. But defeat, which is the shame of men and peoples, is the happiness of women, and nations too that weep and make politics, together they sing and rebel, sell themselves and adapt to other men and other peoples at the feet of other gods."

A mirage of Greece began to spread, land of the South: silence everywhere, barren rocks, white temples, pine trees and islands in the sea. Alexander was speaking:

"The most learned teachings cannot show us moderation in the thirst for conquest or the thirst in our bodies. What thirst is greater than a warrior's after a day of battle? What conqueror can be magnanimous who has never known defeat? I know none with greater valour than the Argyraspides, my Silver Shields, I salute the splendour of their courage, and its anonymity, which raises it above the illusions of reward. Kings, I say to you: unless you are the son of a god, relinquish all thought of empire; empires cannot last unless the conquered elect you their god in the political peace that follows all victory. But what memories are those of battle! The royal chariot and its banners bearing our name draws all the eyes of friend and foe, it cuts at speed through the troops pressed tightly together with lances as far as the eye can see, like the bristles on a boar. You are drunk on the noise of battle, the sight of you revives your weakening soldiers, your audacity hastens victory and a people's loss of freedom, and whether once civilised or barbarian now by your will they are a people of slaves. Unless their own audacity leads them to the path of martyrdom."

In a Latin landscape of villas and cultivated fields, Caesar was coming to the end of his sermon:

"What we have done has been well done. Never doubt yourself. Conquer whenever conquest is possible. How strange to be moved by anything other than the desire for glory. We conquer women and peoples. In the one we lose our hair, in the other the respect of men. But in all things, never concern yourself with the outcome. The Sibylline books are as nothing, the Sibyls are nothing, nor is the flight of the birds. Let every man act with the freedom that is his right, for there is no crime in this world, neither for conquerors nor for adulterers. If you are a king, act like a king. If you are a people, act like a king amongst peoples."

Caesar departed, and the trees at Bois des Buttes began to cry:

"Soldiers! Soldiers of France! Not all the Nine Worthies are dead and some are still to be born. The next died only to be reborn, and to be the king that he was, Arthur, the seventh Worthy. Lend your ear to the sound of his voice." And Arthur spoke:

"Soldiers, be ready to die and be reborn, just as I will be reborn. Death has no meaning, or the round table either, if I must return to rule once more after the death of all my equals. There is a castle with five towers, the one in the middle is surrounded by the other four. The four towers are white and beautiful. But the one in the middle is vermilion. The white towers will fall, the one in the middle will stand. O Britain mine, and O sweet France, learn to predict me and divine the future in me."

Old Emperor Charlemagne walked by, and in the distance sometimes the dying sound of the horn was heard, but it never silenced the sound of machine-gun fire, nor the explosion of shells passing like the rustle of silk, nor the thunder of troops moving out and the clatter of others arriving. And the old emperor wept:

"The truth of war lies in the stillness of the forests, as skilled as the Celts who taught me the rudiments of war. Listen, can you hear the savage song of woodlands on the march?"

The barren and baked landscape of Judea then reappeared and the Ninth Worthy, Godfrey of Bouillon uttered these words:

"Wage war on your knees far from your native land. The hands of the barons are the servants of the earth. The arms of the labourers are the lovers of the earth they fertilise. Girls should not be servants in their own families. The warrior is destined to live far from his native land, in exile and anguish. And death is beautiful in fighting for a just cause. Come, come the night more beautiful than the day!"

And so the Ennead disappeared and its eternal glory shone still in the distance. There was only the appalling sadness of the battlefield left, and the stretcher-bearer kneeling by the wounded was thinking neither of the Nine Worthies nor the danger he was in, he was thinking of Coralie, that slip of a woman he loved, and who loved him also but without constancy. He was sad, so sad he thought he would die, and when he saw his comrade crying for help, he ran to him as quickly as he could and that was the moment he was hit in the chest by a bullet from a machine-gun. He fell dead to the ground without suffering, and the adored name of Coralie died away on his lips.

Anatole, now returned to the present, kissed the hand of Coralie. As they walked along they saw Elvira and Pablo Bluedog kissing near the Montparnasse cemetery.

"Don't look at them," said Anatole to Coralie, and Pablo said to Elvira: "Now that Anatole and Coralie have seen us kissing everyone will know you're my mistress, and there's no reason for you not to come and live with me."

"Come on, Pablo, don't be silly," said Elvira. "Nicolas is coming back from the war tomorrow, he's on the indispensable list, the head doctor at the National Ruritanian Hospital put him there. It's over between us."

"Well, if you're breaking up with me," said Bluedog, "I'll go and see Nicolas's sister and tell her everything."

"You're revolting," said Elvira, "if I'd known how revolting you are I'd never have loved you. I hate you, get away from me!"

And she began to run home, but Pablo Bluedog ran after her and caught up with her as she was ringing for the concierge. There was a violent fight and Elvira would have had to submit if Pablo hadn't slipped and fallen to his knees on the pavement. Elvira grabbed her chance and closed the door behind her, where the concierge had been waiting a good long while.

For the rest of the night all she could hear was Pablo Bluedog drumming on the shutters and shouting in his heavy Spanish accent:

"Elvira, listen, open the door, I love you, I adore you, and if you don't do as I say I'll shoot you with my revolver. I'll tell Nicolas and his sister everything, I swear. Open the door, Elvira! Love is here, with me. Love is peace, and I am love because I'm neutral, but he is war. War isn't love but hate. So you hate him and you love me, my little Elvira. Open the door and let me in, I'm your Pablo and I adore you."

Chapter Eight

"In the first part of 1915, during the Austro-Hungarian assault on G…, an event occurred that was so singular it should be recorded forever in the Annals of Love.

If you'll allow, I won't divulge any names and use only the initials.

The Polish commander of the artillery mounting the assault in that sector was Count P, first cousin of Count C, commander of the opposing Russian artillery. The war has created a number of these distressing situations in families dispersed all over a divided Poland.

Even though "in the service of Austria", Count P was very rich and owned vast estates in the area. He had lived there for many years before the war and had been compelled to leave his companion, a plump shopkeeper with a long body and a voluptuous manner who was also an accomplished musician, and not long since on the best of terms with Count C, the commander of the Russian artillery. As for Count C, his own mistress whom he loved dearly was also behind the lines, she was young and patrician, recently widowed, and having discovered the pleasures of love for the first time was saddened at being separated from her lover. Count P had been introduced to her before he became the enemy and the invader, and had courted her assiduously but vainly. Nonetheless he hadn't forgotten his musician, his shopkeeper in G., and being a musician himself and a talented composer, as a way of reminding himself of her he had the idea of giving a concert, a serenade to be performed at dawn and at dusk, such that no lover had ever attempted before for the delight of his mistress. He captured in his mind the sound of the canon, learned their notes, the timbre and the pitch of their soul, and composed a horrifying symphony which he ordered his battery to perform. His rival the Russian commander, no less a musician than he, understood perfectly – so perfectly that he added the wild tones of his own canon, unfortunately far less powerful, to complete his enemy's ghastly symphony. It was chamber music pure and simple. This death-carrying concert lasted two days and two nights, terrifying those who were listening and would far rather have not, but who could only admire its chilling and magnificent harmony.

During the second night Count P ordered the bombardment of G with shells loaded with suffocating gas, concocted on his command in memory of the Moors of Grenada, using subtle perfumes that bathed the besieged city in the most varied and violent scents, and their defensive trenches were lit up by a wondrous pyrotechnical display of rockets of all colours which went up ceaselessly and quietly died. Almost the entire population of G perished in the concert, along with the Russian garrison and the mistress of Count P, whom he found dead on the body of her lover Count C. As to the latter's own mistress, who until then had resisted the advances of the victor, she had no choice but to give in to his violence, but that very evening she stabbed Count P to death, he had fallen asleep gorged on roast meats and drunk on hydromel mead and hundred-year-old Tokaj wines, at which point a shell from one last burst of fire from the Russian batteries in the distance landed on the castello where the young widow was living and killed her. So at the final chord of this bloody concert there was nothing left of the four Polish lovers."

And Princess Nathalie Teleshkin concluded:

"I read this story in a letter from Russia. Is there anything more precarious than love at any time? Don't be surprised, my dear Pablo, if love is still more precarious in times of war."

She went back to reading one at a time all the letters Elvira had sent Pablo. Since his return Elvira had been seeing her lover Nicolas again and life continued seamlessly. Nicolas was less and less interested in her, and was running with the young actresses that would come and do shows at the Ruritanian Hospital. Elvira was highly offended and far more jealous than she said, she could see the merry-go-round he was on, but he hadn't noticed any of her affairs.

He learned about them from the pen-pal godmother of one of the patient officers in the hospital. She had made advances to Nicolas which he had coldly received, but he had gone out with her a few times and taken her for tea on rue Rivoli. He had even introduced her to Elvira who was now spending half her time at La Coupole with her Pablo Blue-Hands and his friends. But Nicolas had never made up his mind seriously to court the pretty Francine, the wartime pen-pal of Lieutenant Glass-Cross. She was piqued and wanted to accelerate the break-up of Elvira and Nicolas that she had been pushing for, and one day when she was visiting Lieutenant Glass-Cross, her pen-pal godson, she said to Nicolas "You're a cuckold, my friend." She had a fit when he replied "I don't think so", blushing with embarrassment. That very evening, as Lieutenant Glass-Cross was hobbling out of his room humming Cherubino's song from *The Marriage of Figaro*:

I once had a godmother
Oh my heart oh my God what pain in my heart

and still without believing a word of it, Nicolas started a row with Elvira, after which everyone in Montparnasse who knew anything about it wanted them to separate. But Elvira had got it into her head she must keep her Nicolas and denied everything, and then denied everything else of which she was accused. She stopped going to La Coupole and seeing Bluedick who then wrote to her, and incensed she wrote back saying their friendship was over. Half to get her back and half so that Nicolas, who was his friend, should know everything about what she was like, Pablo, who despised women and had only feelings of violence for them, decided to make Nicolas's sister aware of everything, and to stoke up such scandal that any reconciliation would be impossible.

He went to see Princess Teleshkin, told her he loved Nicolas like a brother, and how upset he was to see him hooked up with someone like Elvira. He described her as a dangerous siren to whom he himself had fallen victim, and drew pictures in the air of her having fun with him, with English aviators, American journalists and a medical auxiliary.

When she heard all this, Natasha Teleshkin was overcome with a horribly painful joy. She had wanted Elvira and her brother to separate for a long time, but was afraid Nicolas would live through this inevitable separation only in terrible suffering.

Pablo Dogdick showed her letters Elvira had written him, but they only confirmed the conviction already planted in the Princess's mind, and in themselves they were not compromising. They were friendly and nothing more. Finally, he showed her some his sketches of nudes for which he had used her as a model, and also a naked photo.

Princess Teleshkin needed nothing more to be drowned in her own convictions. She thanked Pablo for the friendship he was showing in respect of her brother, and her anger at Elvira was so great that had she held her in her hands, she would have strangled her there and then, but she could only take revenge on a bouquet her brother's mistress had painted of dazzling pink peonies against a background of sky blue. She slashed it to ribbons and Pablo, who was attracted and charmed by Elvira's talent, could only be saddened by the vandalism he was witnessing.

When Nicolas arrived at tea-time his sister told him every-thing in tragic tones. Pale as death he went straight back to his studio and told Elvira to leave because he knew everything about her carryings-on, that it was pointless to go on denying it, and that Pablo himself had confessed everything. Then he left again so that Elvira could pack her bags and go.

But when he came back he was unable to get in, the key had been left in the lock on the inside and a strong smell of gas was coming through the joints in the door frame. He sounded the alarm and together with the burly concierge he broke down the door. They found Elvira asphyxiating with her head in the oven. Soon the doctor arrived and had the greatest difficulty bringing her back to life. Nicolas forgave her everything, gave credence to all her denials, and as there was in fact nothing to prove that Pablo was telling the truth, Nicolas put his denunciation down to his bitterness at failing to carry her off.

The sketches proved nothing either, they could easily have been the fruits of Pablo's imagination, and as to the photo, Elvira maintained it had been taken in Petrograd. She must have lost the copy Pablo now had in his possession, or again he might have taken it when he came to visit her with her friends one day. In the end there was nothing left of the whole affair other than eight days in bed for Elvira, during which the fake Ovid St Euxine dropped by the studio on rue Maison-Dieu with old Otto Warning.

Warning sensed that Eros was waging a courageous battle with the forces of its opposition, and said to the couple:

"Your love is like a shell that could explode into a thousand pieces with any sudden movement. There's another like it where I live and Moses Ladder does as well. He's a small grey man with a musical body, and at the start of the war he'd been back from America for about six months. He'd met and worked with various people but had come back with only little money, and by mid-August 1914 he had worked through almost all of his savings. It occurred to him to put his overseas connections to use, and he wrote to all and sundry offering war souvenirs and trophies for sale. The replies he received left him in no doubt as to the level of American interest in the struggles of the European armed forces, especially the enemy forces for which there was a general American sympathy, or the success he would have trading in heroic merchandise of this kind. But merchandise was exactly what Moses Ladder lacked. At that time the field of battle was closed to him on health grounds, which is why he had been withdrawn from service, and those on active duty hadn't started sending trophies home yet. Moses Ladder spent the best part of the money he had left in junk shops and markets buying all kinds of antique military objects as cheaply as possible. He picked up French and German helmets from the war of 1870, and everything he could find in bottom-end shops full of rejects from Army Procurement, everything he could lay his hands on in Temple over in the 3rd, like old officer's caps, sabres some of which went back to the Napoleonic Empire, breastplates, shakos, a bearskin hat, a drum, three bugles and a sabretache – they all found its way into his rooms. The high point of his collection was wooden debris from planes aviators had crashed, and which he went to fetch at aerodromes and the shops nearby. He carefully packed up all these objects and sent them to America where they were immediately sold. Almost straightaway he got a telegram back asking him to send more, and so his business couldn't have been more successful and he made a lot of money.

But nothing lasts. The Americans began to see that these old colbacks, pistols and cutlasses, epaulettes and other dead military cast-offs had nothing to do with this war; and if he wanted to keep his American investors Moses Ladder had to work out how to lay his hands on authentic souvenirs from the war that was actually happening. I don't know how, but he managed to get a pass and he accompanied an Italian correspondent on a visit to the front. They went in a car and Moses gathered an ample crop of uniform buttons, German helmets, bayonets, and round *feldgrau* caps. He also picked up an unexploded shell, but on the way back his companion pointed out he might have difficulty getting through the gates of Paris with a piece of kit like that.

And so here's Moses Ladder very forlorn. This shell was going to be the best piece of all – a brand new 77/14 shell! At that time, end of November 1914, there were only very few to be had on the home front and he had been hoping to sell it in America for a thousand dollars. [ill]

But having thought about it a solution soon appeared. They stopped at the next village where he bought a large four-pound loaf and cut it in half. He carefully scooped the bread out from the crust and replaced it with the precious shell, which is how it passed through into the capital. But his tribulations didn't end there, because the very next person he spoke to vigorously explained all the dangers involved in possessing such a device.

"If you send it away, the boat might explode," he was told, "or at least there's all the risk of injury and damage, leave aside that you'll be to blame. The shell must be disarmed and carefully emptied."

Hardly reassured, Moses Ladder went in search of an artilleryman to unscrew the rocket from the shell and empty it. But at Vincennnes the only artillerymen he could find were mechanics.

"You'll need a deputy bomb squad officer," an aged adjutant declared, but despite all his efforts he's been unable to find one, and he lives in a heightened state of permanent anxiety. He's padded it up completely with his underwear and keeps it in his wardrobe. He showed it to me with I don't know how many precautions, and sometimes he wakes up at night with a start, he thinks he's heard some creak in the cupboard and imagines the inauspicious projectile will explode and kill him, and blow up the whole house as well."

Having told the story of the shell with his customary prolixity old Warning departed with a smile, leaving the two lovers together whose feelings had been so profoundly affected by the war.

As she kept running into him, after a time Elvira started chatting with Pablo Bluedog again but said nothing about it to Nicolas Varinov, who was starting to look yellow with anxiety about it all.

Whenever they met Pablo would urge her to come with him, and she began to listen to him favourably once again.

One day the lovely Coralie came to see her and told her about a clairvoyant she admired who read cards as well, and had a number of other ways of seeing the future.

They went together the following day. Madame Adonysia lived in rue Nollet in Batignolles. She had been telling fortunes since the start of the war, having been widowed: her husband was a professor of mathematics who had left her without resources. To distinguish herself from the others, her idea was to call upon St Jean-Marie Vianney of Ars, and also on Papus, the Magus whose real name was Dr Encausse and who had just died. By all accounts these oracles would reply satisfactorily.

There were no men, and only single women were allowed. She placed no advertisements in the newspapers and recruited her clients solely by word of mouth. The cost of a consultation was five francs in advance, and for twenty francs those of her clients she considered the most discreet were admitted to what she called her "highest wartime consultation", which consisted of spreading the powder from a Lebel rifle cartridge and interpreting the figures that emerged.

As Madame Adonysia considered Coralie a reasonable person with plenty of discretion, she was happy to carry out her "highest wartime consultation".

The powder replied that Elvira would leave her current lover for the one who was courting her.

She came home highly affected by this visit. Next morning she woke up early to the sound of a dog howling in the street, she shook Nicolas Varinov who answered with a yawn.

"Can you hear the dog howling?" she said, "it means separation."

He paid her no mind and went back to sleep. But later that day while Nicolas was at his sister's, she ran over to Pablo's and said she was ready to be with him. Pablo exhibited such satisfaction at her decision that straightaway, and just as he did every time he had a new mistress, he took her to a department store and bought her a raincoat which she wore that very evening at La Coupole with her new lover.

The next day, through the offices of Nicolas Varinov, she received all her belongings, her dresses, her fur coats, her painter's gear and her pictures.

But the day after she was already tiring of Pablo. Once again her heart was heavy with love for Nicolas. She wrote to him and he replied, and on the eighth day while Pablo Canouris, also known as Pablo Dogsdick, was strolling in Montmartre, with the help of Coralie she left the studio of the painter with the celestial blue hands, who had not shown the presence of mind to say that his home was now hers and give her the key.

For women of today have a sense of their unique importance as the guardians of social life and the human race, at a time when its male representatives are doing their utmost to annihilate each other. Whether within or outside marriage they have nothing but impatience for the male yoke, they want to be mistress of the destiny of mankind, they give little thought to submission and have an irreversible taste for freedom; and if women are to save the human race, they will certainly need their hands free.

That was the reason why once back with Nicolas Varinov, who by going off to war had failed to maintained his dominion and allowed her to savour her freedom, Elvira's thoughts turned once again to her grandmother Pamela Monsenergues the Mormon, and she concluded that polygamy was of little use in war time or peace time either.

She made up her mind that women, because of their numbers and the freedom they enjoyed from the State, held a power that outstripped the power men would formerly have enjoyed, who by now were in any case enslaved to the nation.

She thought this power would be wonderfully exercised if women concentrated their energy on open polyandry. She took five lovers, which counting Nicolas Varinov made six, whom she treated almost as slaves.

Her chosen ones were a clown from Piedmont whose make-up and multicoloured costume enchanted her; a medical student who saw a future in literature; a man who had lost both arms, who spoke to her brutally and adored her; an aviator on the home front called Panteleimon, he belonged to the Ruritanian contingent and she had picked him because his name reminded of her Madame P, where she had stayed in Petrograd; and lastly a fellow from the North who sang lovely songs.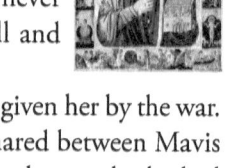

She worked unimaginably hard with the aim of never being dependent on a man. Her paintings sold well and she made a good living.

She played like a Queen the instrument of power given her by the war.

None of her lovers filled her heart, which she shared between Mavis Springer and Coralie, the lovely redhead with the hazel eyes who looked so much like a drop of blood on the blade of a sword.

Chapter Nine

Whereas Elvira was embarked on a reverse Mormonism and doing her utmost to remain infertile, when for the protection and the honour of society a pointed interest in procreation might have been thought a woman's duty, Anatole only had thoughts of founding a new religion.

Disappointed in Coralie, now an adornment in Elvira's seraglio, Anatole looked upon his life and times if not with contempt, then with an astonishment and a severity mixed horror.

Such thoughts as well as his natural inclinations lead him to imagine a religion devoted to honour, about which he spoke at length one day to the fake Ovid soon after he had been discharged from service. He hardly left the house, and spent his time pondering how to organise his life and make good his plans.

Anatole Holybest lived in rue Delambre in the same house as Otto Warning, in a room thinly partitioned from Moses Ladder's. Anatole Holybest welcomed Ovid St Euxine with every appearance of joy, and started saying straightaway:

"You should think of me as a sort of monk. I'm devoting my life or what's left of it to completing my mission.

My plan is to found a religion without dogma and without priests, and whose vocation is the moral and physical education of children. You may say it's an idea that could only occur to a soldier and you'd be right. I was a soldier and in my soul I've remained one. The renewal of the religious idea everywhere is deceptive, in reality all religion is practically extinct and has become utterly vague. These days superstition and religious belief blinker the mind so much that you're a cleverer man than I if you can disentangle them, in a religion or anywhere else.

Today we're witnessing something not seen since the Roman Empire and the end of paganism: the faithful following a religion, supporting it, defending it, honouring it, but not believing in it. As you know the commonplace is literally true that says the people need a religion, but now people question their beliefs without necessarily being any the happier. Disinterested faith is rare these days and will only become more so, or else connect to the vaguest beliefs, or else collapse entirely into the worst and the most lunatic superstitions. Antoinism from Belgium, Rasputinism and the other mystic madnesses from Russia, not to mention all the absurdities that erupt every day from the four corners of the earth, they're all so many examples of the idiocies that spring from the soul of the people even in such a controlled state as France. And let's not forget the convulsionaries of Saint-Médard, to speak of something more than just the contemporary. A religion of honour would spare informed people all these pipe dreams. Above all it eliminates the fairy tales of atonement and reward which are the most dangerous inventions of the founding fathers of religion. Honour has always been a rare kind of superiority granted to certain people. They meet on the field of battle and scarcely anywhere else. There's a lot to say, but basically it can be argued that a sense of honour has all but disappeared from the face of the earth, apart from a few outstanding cases and those that, without wishing to diminish them, stem from necessity, such as war.

Religions promised everyone rewards in the next world, and sociologists promised individuals happiness in this one. All that must be done away with, people must find happiness in themselves, in the satisfaction of doing their duty and safeguarding their honour. With strong and true education, we can succeed in that. Think of Charles Fox, he promised his son he would take him to see the destruction of a wall. When he learnt the wall had been taken down, he ordered it rebuilt and blown up a second time so as not to break his word. This famous orator had a sense of honour, and refused to distort his son's future sense of it by breaking his own promise.

We need to glorify the great acts of honour of our times, and sing their praises as the norm rather than the exception."

The fake Ovid Saint-Euxine politely interjected that Mr Émile Faguet had entertained an adjacent idea in the last chapter of his book, *The Abdication of Morality*.

"Morality, I grant you," replied Anatole Holybest, "but what I'm talking about is religion. Of all the rites and rituals, I want the act of suicide to be the most significant. I think it's outstandingly moral and outstandingly redemptive. Let everyone who's failed in their duty kill themselves, without fuss or fear.

You're not following. Even after several years of war we hardly know anything about death, and still less about dying.

Everyone should have their own honour, the soldier as much as the bandit, and the parliamentarian as much as the trader. Highwaymen used to have their own honour to which they adhered, but nowadays criminals are without honour. Nowadays bankruptcy involves little dishonour either, and very few businessmen filing for bankruptcy ever commit suicide."

"But isn't suicide considered an offence, or even a sin?" Ovid queried.

"Quite possibly, but how beautiful when sin comes from following your honour."

Taking him over to the table by the window where he was writing Anatole Holybest went on:

"I'm tired of being alone, when I was with soldiers I knew long hours of loneliness away from women. Women don't love me anymore and I don't mean anything to them. Coralie has left me, and for Elvira as well. Absolutely. Elvira and her harem of men and women. The lovely redhead I loved should be called No Man's Land now, you'll forgive me for using the expression, it comes from the Tommies, my brothers in arms. Come and see her with me, after which I'll know what it is honour demands from me, and if I'm to be a martyr to honour, then I'm ready."

He got dressed and they went over to Coralie's who greeted them coldly, and went on arranging roses in a jug.

This is what our poet said to her:

"Coralie, come back to me... I love you like you were the daughter of King Maghmoor of Spain. An Irish poet says her family was not an obscure one and that she married Eocaid, King of Ireland and son of Duach. What wouldn't you do for me if I were Hammurabi from Babylon, the great and good legislator? May God bring them both back to earth, perhaps they would love each other, King Hammurabi and the daughter of King Maghmoor.

Please stop smelling those roses and listen to me. Isn't what a man has to say worth the scent of a rose? Your eyes are like gin at the bottom of the glass of a drunk. Put your hands down, those flowers are evil, they're faithless and pitiful and they're losing their petals. I can hear singing outside, perhaps it's Lilith wailing, there's no redemption for her maternal despair. As though there were any despair but the despair of loving for the sake of love alone. The song is making you smile, but if I were close to a sea I'd believe in the halcyon song, it's death to anyone who hears it. You can put your hands over your ears all you like, anyway we're not by the sea, but if I were closer than I care to imagine I'd kill you even without the halcyon song, and then I'd kill myself, it'd be as though the halcyon were singing for us both.

You don't believe me. Tragedies like that happen every day, nobody cares. Separated for all eternity, or united, which is exactly the same. Nobody cares. And nobody comes back, believe me. Ever. I use to think that some of them came back. But it was a mistake. You've never seen a corpse. I saw one who was bald like men on the island of Mykonos in the Cyclades. They buried him, but on the third day it was clear he had risen to suck the blood of a girl who wouldn't love him. He took a liking to it, and varied his pleasures by sucking the blood of a different young woman every night. You look surprised but it's nothing new, in Hungary a few centuries ago there were large numbers of vampires. In the end the one I'm talking about was exhumed and the grave-diggers cut off his head. He's been quiet since then, but I never believed the bald soldier had survived anyway, and I think the girls were inventing ways to explain the love bites they'd got from their boyfriends.

It's getting dark, I can't see your hands or your mouth, only your eyes like alcohol on fire. You're no more than a shadow, and I'm not even a shadow. You can't see me. You can't imagine me. We're separated by the sea, the treacherous sea, treacherous like you, sometimes the halcyon flies over and sings the song of death, except when it nests at the winter solstice. Don't you ever have those halcyon days that calm even the sea? I'd like to have been a ship's pilot on those days.

I'd like to conquer you, captives like conquerors, but I've been at war too long to believe in conquests and I think they're impossible."

He kissed Coralie's hand and left, never to see her again. She spoke not a word. Ovid St Euxine said goodbye in the street, not without reproaching him for the outrageous things he had said to Coralie, or so he thought. And Anatole Holybest went back to where he lived in rue Delambre.

He could hear the voices of Moses Ladder and Otto Warning through the partition. He heard the words shell, explosion, artificer, expeditions to America; and Ladder was clearly saying: "I've had it here far too long, I'm going to get rid of it today, now. Too bad."

"Those people always struck me as wrong," thought Anatole Holybest. "They're spies scheming to blow up some building central to the defence of the nation."

He began to listen still more closely. Moses Ladder was saying: "I'll do what I did to get it here. I bought a 4-lb loaf, scooped it out and put my live shell into it. And now God's will be done…"

"What a vile individual," thought Anatole Holybest. "The same precautions to get a bomb in and then get it out again, it all shows this brigand's abominable plots. Honour dictates the prevention of this crime."

Anatole Holybest took his hat and his revolver and went down into the street to wait for Moses Ladder, who soon after appeared on his own with the 4-lb loaf under his arm. He walked towards the Montparnasse viaduct where he left his 4-lb loaf. But at that moment Anatole Holybest jumped on him and cried:

"Loathsome spy, you'll not blow up the viaduct!"

Moses Ladder defended himself, but in a vicinity where there was no-one to cry to for help Anatole Holybest threw him to the ground and rained blows on him, and with each one a strangely musical sound rose from the body of Moses Ladder.

As he fought he touched the loaded revolver through the clothes of Anatole Holybest and tried everything to get a hold of it. Using all his cunning he finally managed it. He fired a deadly shot into his opponent, who was still able to grab his wrist, wrestle the weapon from him and shoot him twice in the head. And he died on the body of Moses Ladder.

Meanwhile Otto Warning was saying to Egon Allemanic who had come to see him:

"That idiot Moses Ladder has just left with his shell hidden in a loaf. He was so afraid the device would blow up, his life was a plague. He's going to leave it somewhere and soon everyone will be crying Bosch attack. Moreover we were making enquiries through our friend Heinzmann in Zürich, which were quite proper and indeed proving fruitful. But our prudence and our bonhomie will ensure we remain above suspicion, I know."

The next morning two bodies were found embracing each other. There was a 4-lb loaf close by with a 77/14 shell inside.

When she heard of the death of Anatole Holybest Coralie said to Elvira:

"I knew he was going to die, he said things to me yesterday that belonged more to the next world than a man enjoying life."

They were in Elvira's studio. Nicolas was in attendance along with Panteleimon the aviator, the clown, and the student who saw a future in literature.

Elvira was sitting at her easel and as he looked at her, Nicolas thought of the seated woman, the Seated Helvetia on the coin of his youth you had to be careful not to accept.

He smiled at her and thought, "Elvira will exist forever. She's like all women, and the epitome of all women. She's fake like the seated woman on a fake five-franc Swiss coin."

And as "a seated woman" in a time of "standing men", Elvira's thoughts turned to the lasting pleasures of weakness and the benefits of artifice.

A note on the text

The text of *La Femme assise* I've translated into English is the one established by Michel Décaudin, the editor in French of Apollinaire's prose works: Guillaume Apollinaire, *Œuvres en prose*, Éditions Gallimard (Bibliothèque de la Pléiade), volume 1, Paris, 1977. Décaudin was joined by Pierre Caizergues in editing the further two volumes of the Pléiade edition of Apollinaire's work in prose, which were published in 1991 and 1993. To read the editorial work of both Caizergues and Décaudin, and Décaudin's edition is particular of *La Femme assise*, is to be immersed in the kaleidoscope of plans in Apollinaire's constant experimentation and his thought constantly on the go. It's tempting to look for moments of breakage in his life and work, attempts at breaking with the past, because just like his poetry Apollinaire's prose fiction adopts, develops and evolves into a multitude of seemingly incompatible forms. And yet there's the continuity in his writing of a person seeking consistently to make sense of the world and of what he has to offer his readers in response. There's no suggestion of the slate of history being wiped clean, or of any point to such an ambition. Instead there's an ever-present confusion of past and present, a constant search for illumination not only of *what* we see and read, but *how*. Décaudin has traced the various projects and drafts that flowed into the composition of *La Femme assise*, suggesting in the process how the novel was hastily completed to a deadline before being published by Éditions de la Nouvelle Revue Française in 1920, after Apollinaire's death in the flu epidemic on 9 November 1918. After measured investigation Décaudin concluded that the typescript used for that first publication is the copy held in the Bibliothèque Jacques-Doucet in Paris of an original now lost; and this copy is the typescript he used for his edition of the book in volume 1 of Apollinaire's complete prose works. In translating the narrative, Décaudin's notes and comments, which range from the informative to the speculative, have been a constant companion to me. There's been the continuous pleasure, however digressive, of reading pages that once had a place in Apollinaire's text but were subsequently discarded, and the ever-renewed insight into Apollinaire's sense of narrative shape and purpose. More than that still, what emerges from Décaudin's work and the many paths he's gone down, is that in assembling this narrative full of wit and fantasy, Apollinaire remains fundamentally concerned with accuracy and documented reality – biographical, anecdotal, historical, geographical, cultural, institutional. What better way to show the effects of illusion than in silent, meticulous detail? Rather magically, that silence is given a voice by the editorial work of Décaudin, which then silently supported me as I wrote this translation. I hope it bears witness to what in 1924 Paul Dermée called this 'unique and incomparable book'.

The Story Re-told

Memoir of a translation

I

Imagine a gashing wound. Imagine a wound suffered by a dashing though rather portly lieutenant in the Foreign Legion. Imagine him wounded in the head and calling it the arm, in salutation of another damaged poet whose generosity he faulted. Imagine him befriending a painter with blue hands launching himself into painting on the winds of the blue. Imagine an art devoted to understanding the meaning of study and blown apart by WW1. Imagine fearless living lost in deathly confusion. Imagine the confusion of rips and tears and voices shattered like shrapnel shattering. Imagine shards of voice without the magic of breaking to make, and instead a hundred deafnesses and blindnesses each lost in their own hearing and seeing. Imagine living when so many have died and been killed. Imagine joy confused in complacency or the other way around. Imagine inventing the ease and the freedom to shape and fashion, to give birth to all things, and still being still stuck in an image of invention. Imagine war giving birth to despair, and then imagine a study of despair in the language of glee. Imagine the protection of an inner world as the only gift people are willing to accept. Imagine inventing utopias for the sake and the beauty of others but enclosing others still further. Imagine the joy of study confused with the joy of cages, all in the name of study. Imagine the volatility of eyes and ears and vocal chords fluttering over the crests of confusion. Imagine rust and poison mixing the colours of living. Imagine the currencies of delusion and poetry confused.

And then imagine listening to a music made of scattered memories, a music alive and dissolving in the confusion of the moment. And now imagine our own moment absorbed as well in a past to which it is lovingly and brutally deaf. Imagine the obliteration of words offered in words, the words of a specific ocean drowning in their own specific ocean. Or imagine something else entirely. But looking back at it in this moment, such is how I imagine my time translating *Seated Woman* by Guillaume Apollinaire, the last text he wrote before dying in 1918 of the "Spanish" flu that incubated during the war, the aftermath of which he evokes with wit, purpose and the silence of grief, natural and man-made catastrophes woven together. In re-joining life at the point of death, Apollinaire finds a vein of writing from which gushes both psychological and political trauma. And yet confidence is rekindled in looking and hearing, and he writes with words that fly if only they belong to you and any reader now. As though to speak grief, destruction and disaster, as well as love, only the words of others will do. And I imagine translating as catching up with the capacity we all share to give shape to the unknown multitudes we carry within.

II

You see that I've no other way to draw you into, or back into the world of Guillaume Apollinaire than to try and say something about why it's important to me. Not just me, me, me, but more because like so much powerful art, Apollinaire's mission is to draw people into themselves, and from there outwards again. I'm taking an oblique approach to presenting him, even though translating might suggest something immediate in the relation with a text and another language, at least as something tactile as tactile as anything to do with words can be. Despite its many and varied elements what's striking about Apollinaire's writing, including art writing, is his constant search for simplicity. It springs from a conviction that adventurous art comes to life in the moments where human beings interact.

Many of the people that populate Apollinaire's imagination as he researched and composed *Seated Woman* are drawn from the loose community of artists that populated his life and memory, and that largely made up the European avant-garde of his generation that he was so centrally involved in. "Drawn from": loosely evoked, even caricatured, rather than slavishly reproduced. But if there's criticism involved it's one that punctures his own complacency as well, and his narrators', of which there are quite a few, and ultimately the complacency in all of us. In this story perhaps more than anywhere Apollinaire is searching for openness, and a freedom of relation between people that seems all too often beyond our reach. Perhaps that's the source of the strange and moving combination here as everywhere in his writing of melancholy and optimism. I'd call it lyrical, even in prose, because of its shape and its sweep. Not a weepy lyricism or an idealising one either, it interrogates our inwardness rather than simply luxuriating in it. It's a lyricism that wonders about seeing and hearing beyond the points of view we inhabit, or that invade us.

Max Jacob or his avatar Moses Ladder is one of those who comes into the story as though immediately about to leave again. And yet he returns after what seems a life time, and a life-time of war. Apollinaire's evocation of him starts off as a shard in the kaleidoscopic image he fashions of Paris during World War 1. He threads together an aura of a capital city and capital of art that's at once appealing, indulgent, and troubling – even distressed at times, you might think, if there were a voice that emerged securely enough to know its own grief. Distress is dispersed everywhere, it seems to belong to everyone and no-one, but so does wit, generosity and energy. Like Apollinaire, Max Jacob arrived in Paris in the early 1900s, the time of the twilight of Symbolist poetry and the dawn of avant-gardism, when art-forms pushing at the limits of inwardness suddenly burst free, as though there weren't a limit between inner and outer at all. Suddenly modern life seemed all you needed to sweep away the cobwebs of inhibition and self-censorship. Very few seemed to see the war coming or the events of 1914–1918 that so horrified some while energising others, and Max Jacob began to compose poems that after the war he thought Surrealism had benefitted from, and which had the ambition not only to disrupt the world through any number of chance encounters, but change the whole way we imagine it, its possibilities and disasters.

Back just before the end of the war in 1918, Apollinaire had himself coined the word 'surréel' or surreal in the introduction to his explosive play *Parade*, and again in his *Les Mamelles de Tirésias*, *The Breasts of Tiresias*, or Tiresias's udders or his nipples, which later Poulenc turned into an opera, with music of a very different kind from the chamber music made of cannon fire which readers hear towards the end of *Seated Woman*, in Chapter Eight. Jacob mixed the high-octane life-style of avant-garde artists before and after Work War 1 with the demands of his conversion from Judaism to Catholicism, regardless of which he was murdered at Drancy by the Nazis in 1944. Much of his poetry both before and after World War 1 was published after Apollinaire died in 1918 but like in Pablo Picasso, Apollinaire had found a kindred poetic spirit. With his strangely prescient antennae, it's easy to imagine Apollinaire sensing the distress and the vision of Jacob's satirical play with word association and historical allusion. Still, Apollinaire's own avatar in *Seated Woman*, as refracted a version of himself, just like the others in the novella, has a very different path through the War from Jacob's. In the story the two become embroiled in a deadly stand-off made of pantomime and melancholy, or order and adventure, to coin Apollinaire's own phrase – which here morphs into mess of fantasy and chaos, involving disconnection and suspicion everywhere.

Blaise Cendrars also figures in disguise; the name is itself a pseudonym and once again it's an avatar who speaks in *Seated Woman*. I alluded to him at the beginning, and Apollinaire continues the play of lost and found and lost again by confusing the wounds each suffered in the war. It was Cendrars who lost his right arm in the Somme in 1915, whereas Apollinaire was invalided out of active service in 1916, with a shrapnel wound to the head that required trepanation. Echoes and affinities cast their lines not only into the past and back again, but from side to side, and into the future, for those still there to pick them out. And yet these affinities seem also to kick over their traces.

One of my motivations in translating *Seated Woman* was to follow paths of a mind in a culture, the to-and-froing between an individual and a collective that are so elaborate that often they need to be shown rather than told. I wanted to explore my sense of translating as capable of this kind of showing, or linguistic miming, and the sense that it isn't only the meaning of words that translation can give to hear, but also the kinds of invitation that texts can offer, invitations to engage, and perhaps to cross over into the uncertain and the insecure. They come from Apollinaire himself and many other writers, and with the help of reading and translating, I hope his voice will begin to infiltrate the distressed times that are our own.

Cendrars played his own part in the explosive modernism of pre-War Paris, and during his life-as time the Second World War inexorably followed on from the First, he was attached to the British Expeditionary Force during the German invasion of France in 1940. How radically his mentality will have changed in the intervening period between 1918 and 1939, as an artist committed to some kind of moral understanding of war. In 1914 he joined the Foreign Legion and was encouraging other artists to enlist. By the 1920s he was abandoning poetry in favour of novels and novellas, hoping to connect with reality in more immediate and urgent ways. And already in his 1926 novel *Moravagine*, the name of whose eponymous hero combines sex, birth and death in French, he was exploring psycho-social fantasies of utopia, supposedly achieved by revolution or psychiatry as well as war.

Once again it's difficult not to admire Apollinaire's prescience, his openness to artistic colleagues and rivals, his understanding of the pressures they lived with and that produced their many creativities. In *Seated Woman* the living ghost of Cendrars appears as a former soldier in the guise as a poet at once exotic and fake, fixated at times, acting as a minimal facilitator of the unfolding events and a rather pontificating observer. But in *Seated Woman*, Apollinaire's own earlier story of socially-minded aspiration and chaos, written eight years earlier than *Moravagine* and while still in the thick of it, how many others besides Cendrars appear enclosed within their own skin, eyes and ears? In his own story of war-time futility and generosity combined, Apollinaire seems to sense in Cendrars, his rather competitive comrade-in-arms and art, a search for a comprehensive understanding of life. The real Cendrars and his avatar the fake Ovid refract each other playfully, perhaps also inaccurately, in any case symbolically, in this indulgent little satire. Apollinaire exposes all the artifice of system and formula, offers them back to his reader in shards, in search for a more intuitive understanding of human society.

III

But what is the new art and the art of the new that so appealed to Apollinaire, and which in turn he so energised? Picasso features overwhelmingly, even though in *Seated Woman* his avatar, the painter with blue hands, is fashioned in a mixture of admiration, perplexity, anxiety, and even a mistrust resulting, perhaps, from Apollinaire's first-hand experience of war and human destruction. What a stand-off there is in this story between optimism and despair. The key to it all, it seems, is the growing conviction that humanity is limited in its vision; and that its capacity and its ambition to imagine a world beyond its own understanding is flawed by the tyrannies of the point of view.

This tyranny begins with formal experience of it, which for artists amounts to first-hand experience. Since the Renaissance, and by now as matter of habit, perspective had signalled the power of the mind to map, plot, reveal and illuminate the world; to organise it, and testify to a viewer's capacity grasp of it. The practice of perspective allowed everything to be placed and re-placed, and relations between things and people to be fashioned in line with a person's experience, sensations, and life. A line in perspective from here to the horizon offers a sighting of a person's place in the world, within a picture and in partnership with looking at one. It offers the imaginary capacity to changing places moment by moment, step by step in any direction, with all the changing relations involved.

But perspectives in succession don't make a whole, and nor do styles. And as Picasso moves through his blue and his pink periods in the years 1901 to 1905, past performances seem to weigh very heavily, and the jugglers and other performers in these pictures begin to show fading artistry and failing memory. Audiences have dwindled to nothing, past skill, gesture, tonality, vision and invention are all going unrecognised and unwanted. In pictures in blue and pink, Picasso shows art in need of an art to show what art can show.

He and his friends were by no means the first to draw on the metropolis as confirmation of the capacity they were looking for to know more than what is already known. Every lived moment belongs to others as well as itself, and in *Seated Woman* Apollinaire draws on the art and politics of nineteenth-century France and America, on the mythologies and phantasmologies underpinning his own modernity of art and war, and his ambitious and melancholic understanding of it. In *Le Peintre de la vie moderne*, *The Painter of Modern Life* of 1863, Charles Baudelaire writes that crowds in the city are like a kaleidoscope with the gift of a mind. He imagines an art aimed at discovering just such a mind, and giving it its freedom: a mind that doesn't think only in lines, whether they join or not, but in simultaneous elements that coincide, refract, reorientate, reshape, explode, rediscover, and reveal the foundational elements of perception and the mind.

The panoramic novels in the nineteenth century of Balzac and Hugo, and the twentieth-century ones of Proust, Joyce, Woolf and Döblin join with other arts of the city in pursuing representations of life lived simul-taneously in space and time. In the poetry and visual art between 1907 and 1914, to embrace the simultaneity of life is a both a practice and an objective, each hand in glove with the other. Picasso's unveiling in 1907 of *Les Demoiselles d'Avignon* not only challenged but explored the conventions of seeing on at least three interlocking levels. In its professed subject matter of the brothel, itself a return to the impressionism of Degas and Toulouse Lautrec, it called to question once again the ideology of viewing pleasure and consumption. It further called out the position of Picasso's likely viewers by forcing evocations of African cultures into the frame, shoving the lines, shapes, associations and heritages of Euro-centric art off pedestal. And the optimism of the whole enterprise is underpinned by form – formal play, formal impatience, formal disruption, formal interrogation and dismissal of perspective, and the vision perspective not so much allows as imposes.

Perspective from the Renaissance to Impressionism offers understanding, even illumination by placing people, and the things that matter to them, in relation to each other along lines that stretch and meet at the horizon: a very changeable horizon, but still a reachable one. But here was an art offering not to place things at all, but set them free; offering to displace things, and viewers with them; to see things from more than one place at once, the front, the back, the sides, all the faces of a cube.

 Louis Vauxcelles coined the term cubism in 1908, in response to new pictures Georges Braque showed in 1908 at Daniel-Henry Kahnweiler's gallery, which did so much to support this art. Vauxcelles used the word to accuse the paintings of an obsession with geometry and a kind of anti-human divisionism, divisiveness  and reductionism. Vauxcelles had form: in 1905 he'd already labelled Matisse, Vlaminck and Derain 'fauves', 'beasts', by contrast with the somehow pure sophistication of Donatello, the Florentine Renaissance sculptor of the human form and human sensuality. But through its painterly explosions from 1908 into 1912 or so, the spirit of 'cubist' art isn't divisive but inclusive, and immediately practitioners espoused the insult and turned it to their advantage. What's abstract, pointless and bestial to some is visceral, existential and necessary to others; and Apollinaire was at every juncture sensitised to the effects of projection and counter-projection, nowhere more so than in *Seated Woman*. In Cubism it isn't only not only the geometric faces and facets of objects that are depicted at once, but the eclecticism of the world at large, with different things and words and people being brought together, waiting for viewers to give them material sense and inward purpose. The message of Cubism, then? What cube?! Stop previewing viewing! And instead begin again.

At the same time it already wasn't enough. In a coup hardly imaginable these days in relation to an art movement, Filippo Marinetti had his *Manifeste du futurisme*, his futurist manifesto published on the front page of *Le Figaro* in 1909. Even though like all newspapers of the time the pages consisted largely of columns set side by side quite haphazardly, the publication was an event and a happening anticipating many others to come, not only Futurist ones but Dada ones later, but still a time when art was still to spread its wings and fly towards performance art. The speed of a car was championed as far more powerful than the valedictory, classical *Winged Victory of Samothrace*, on prominent display in the Louvre since 1884. An overriding idea of the speed was being trumpeted, combining industry with communication by telegraph, and  merging with the speed of words yet to be invented that would communicate with no connecting wires, grammatical or metaphorical threads, or strings attached at all. An ideal of immediacy was taking off that would wipe clean time and the mind. The future was now present and the present our future.

What an astonishing belief in the power of art to break art; and not only art but the attachments that organise viewing it and the world beyond. For Futurists it wasn't now enough to plot lines and focal points, like in Tintoretto's *Last Supper* in the Church of San Trovaso in Venice, taken at random, or at least without explanation of whatever is taking me there now; and certainly wasn't enough either, like Braque was, to be  mixing the front and the back of guitars, or jug-handles and bicycle wheels and letters borrowed from newspaper headlines. Not lines but frames could now be broken, it seems; broken and dispensed with – frames that not only place people in space but impose situations on them, manipulating all kinds of myth for value and profit. Not just frames of vision and perception could now be escorted from the scene, but the entwinements of psyche and society.

Soon the stunning naivety of such an enterprise was clear; or least the way it was conceived, for the desire can only continue, and the present absorbs the past in any case. In London Percy Wyndham Lewis, marshalling others such as Henri Gaudier-Brzeska and Jacob Epstein had been getting his Vorticism movement going, and in 1914 and 1915 published the visual-verbal, font-smashing, page-refashioning journal which he named *Blast*: partly to express an imperative to blow up all complacency, and partly to champion  the energy of blast furnaces that he wanted society to embrace. In any case he wanted more than imitation, more than fascination with appearance, with the way the modern world looked, and the meek impressionism of what Futurist art now seemed to offer. He wanted a re-structuring.

Apollinaire had been continuing to steer his own way. There's a lightness of touch that drives his insight and the way he seems to grasp the world with his senses as much as his mind, which I wanted to hold on to in the various ways I've translated his writing in this book. In his talk called 'L'esprit nouveau et les poètes', or 'Poets of the New Mentality' that he gave after his return from the front, he wanted to make his own distinction between the modern and the new: between following and leading, and between imitating and imagining. His idea and practice of simultaneity is both lyrical and self-emptying, with equal love it nurtures a voice and interrogates the limits of any voice. Let's see how it is we see, hear and understand, he seems to insist, before we presume to break the frames of the moment, and the lines of our history that are still obscure to us.

In the years from about 1912 to when he joined up in 1914, Apollinaire fashions his poetry of the new, rather than just the modern, in a kind of continuous refractive reference to what he calls Orphism. This is another word he has coined, and while it's become a term in art history it acts more like the aura of a term, or the glow of one – just as Apollinaire would have liked. A word used to evoke an art of the now, and art that illuminates the now, is given a name derived from the figure in Greek mythology, Orpheus, whose singing is associated with the origin of all poetry. An art of the present involves an understanding of history and the past, it seems. And it also involves the physiology of seeing.

IV

Just as the neo-Impressionist or *pointilliste* painters had not so long before, the artists Robert Delaunay and Sonia Delaunay-Terk had become drawn to the work of the chemist Michel-Eugène Chevreul, whose name is inscribed on the Eiffel Tower along with seventy-two other French scientists. His work as a chemist had far-reaching medical implications, but it was particularly his work on colour and the perception of colour that drew the fascination of painters. In his surrealist text of 1926, *Le Paysan de Paris, Paris Peasant*, Louis Aragon remarks that it's the destiny of powerful thought to be reduced to clichés, and wonders whether all that's generally remembered about Darwin is the dictum that man is descended from the apes. The complexity of Chevreul's experimentation and speculation on the performance of colour was similarly reduced, but also mediated, translated if you like, into a working principle. If light through a prism refracts into the primary colours of the rainbow, then primary colours attract each other and complement each other in an interplay of contrasts. Light itself is what mattered to artists now: light made and continually renewed in this dynamic relation of contrasts between primary colours. Contrast and complementarity and contrast are inseparable, and their interaction produces the light by which we see.

The title of Sonia Delaunay-Terk's *Contrastes simultanés* of 1912 and the visual journey it offers shows the extent of the inspiration artists continued to derive from Chevreul's insights into light. The following year, together with Cendrars she created the picture-poem *La Prose du transsibérien et de la petite Jehanne de France*. Her primary colours in gouache and water colour make abstract shapes which unwind through the text of Cendrars's free verse poem. Sixty of these aesthetic artefacts were produced through Cendrars's own publishing venture, Éditions des hommes nouveaux, or New People Publications. Simultaneity of contrasting colours has been developed into a collaboration of word and image which drives and fashions the book.

And yet in many ways the contrast involved in this book, in fact a long sheet which folds unfolds vertically, is more like a clash and a crash. Delaunay-Terk's freedom and optimism of hand and paint seems at odds as much as in partnership with Cendrars's words of psychic constraint, war, civil war, starvation and devastation. The verse charts an odyssey from Paris through pre-Revolutionary Russia and back again, but there is no booty to bring home, nor oppression conquered, no new society established either. Instead there is the triumph of legend itself and its hold on the imagination and the mind. Delaunay comes to that sense of things himself in *Le Poète Assassiné* published in 1916, and digs still deeper into the way myth not only explains but fashions the mind in *La Femme assise* written in 1918, after he was invalided out of the infantry and before he died of the flu in the epidemic. It was published posthumously in 1920.

But if his melancholy steers him into many grief-storms for the loss of lovers, friends, ideas, even generosity itself, his lyricism keeps him open to solidarity and generosity. In developing his Orphism Apollinaire was especially drawn to Robert Delaunay, and in 1912 he wrote a poem in and some prose-poetic art writing that seemed to give Orphism the fullness that comes from giving without keeping. Unlike the collaboration by superimposition of Cendrars and Sonia Delaunay, of darkness on light, Apollinaire's poem and Robert's paintings form a duet with neither in the same place. One is a poem, the other a series of paintings, and each reaches to the other across over a space waiting to be filled with voices waiting to be heard.

Each offering has the title *Les Fenêtres, The Windows*. What windows? Looking out from where and onto what? Physical questions combine with metaphysical ones, and the aesthetic with the ethical. Which point of view combines with which other, or which absorbs the other? Which is lost and which is found? Delaunay paints the frames of seeing as much as what is framed in seeing. There is no single frame highlighted, nor is there any frame within a frame either. Instead frames are everywhere, indistinguishable from the light we see and see by: it's a simultaneity of the illuminated and the illuminating. Delaunay has taken the Cubist optimism of combined perspectives, combined points of view and combined understanding and taken it out to the world, beyond interiors and rooms and into the light. And beyond the object, he invites his viewers into an illumination of dominant symbols as well.

Colour is what we see. When we see light, we see colour. Colour is what we see but it also gives form to how we see – at least how we see light. But light is everywhere. And so for the painter Robert the poet Guillaume, and in the distanced tandem of their practice, how we see light comes to embody what we make of it, and how we make the seeing that is ours. The aspiration is not just to see new, contemporary and modern things, but to see differently, to be illuminated by newness itself. In one painting especially, the Eiffel Tower is integrated in the play of colour contrasts, emerging from it and absorbed in it simultaneously. It's a painting in light and sight of this iconic moment in European modernism and techno-optimism, built for the 1889 *Exposition Universelle* as a monument to solidarity and industrial progress. In Delaunay's painting this monument to engineering, with hardly any purpose other than the radio transmission aerial on the top of it, shows dynamism itself.

At least in the imagination. Always in the fibres Apollinaire's writing is his sense of humility, without which there is neither dynamism nor invention, and instead a rush to immobility and the fantasies of dominion. The dynamism of life, like history, rushes at individuals in ways they may never control, and invention may breathe the same air as frenetic emulation. But by keeping word and image apart, especially his words and Delaunay's imagery, Apollinaire allows each to speak in their own voices and signs. Translation is similarly faithful by keeping its distances and relishing them.

Apollinaire's window-poem is a conversation-poem, as he calls it, with voices from different places combining yet still kept apart, refracting each other across the distances separating them. The place of the poem and of you and me reading it never combine or coalesce, and yet still the poem is held together, making voice out of the dissolution of voice, and connection from vulnerability.

Vulnerability and generosity combine. 'The Windows' shows frames disappearing but also attachments, the loss of which stifles as much as a frame indefinitely imposed. Apollinaire's disappearing Orphic window frames move beyond the misreading of Cubist simultaneity, and the idea that its ambition is to transcend the singularity of someone's point of view. The point of view can't be transcended, it's made of many different lines and associations woven together from the earliest age and compressed in the moment. Such is a person – and the source of the lyricism of Cubism and some of its melancholy. Apollinaire imagines an Orphism that is still lyrical, that still addresses that boundless internal simultaneity, but leaves melancholy behind.

At least for the moment. His Orphism is a poetry that opens itself to the world while dismissing the grandiloquent adoration of appearance in the name of progress, which Apollinaire came to see as the only offering of Futurism. He wanted Orphism to be an art of invention, not just modernity or even novelty; and art that opens the eye and the ear, the body and the mind to their own dawning, their own generation, and their power to create. Not a god-like creation from nothing; but a human creation able to see the light that's given to humans to see.

Apollinaire's window-poem in free verse opens 'like an orange', he writes, 'the beautiful fruit of light'. His poem travels to this embrace of the world from places of darkness, obscurity and trauma: from singularity to solidarity. A poem of human society in all its dimensions, the *there* as well as the *here*, and dedicated to the yet-to be-discovered and known. And yet a poem that's rooted in how we see, not just what. In *Les Peintres cubistes: méditations esthétiques, Aesthetic Meditations on Cubist Painters*, Apollinaire addresses not just Cubism but the whole range of his generation's artistic avant-garde. It's a book that comprises commissions for different occasions as well as extended passages composed especially, which gives it an overall sense of spontaneity combined with depth – an invitation to think poetically. And Apollinaire writes that 'avant tout, les artistes sont des hommes qui veulent *devenir* inhumains. Ils cherchent péniblement les traces de *l'inhumanité*', that 'artists are above all people who want to become inhuman. Painfully they seek traces of *inhumanity*.'

What a wonderful inhumanity this is, that seeks itself within the human, and that humans seek within themselves both painstakingly and painfully. Nothing transcendent then, in the sense of some mock-heroic discarding of everything we think we know, every fantasy we think we can identify, and pinning all our hopes on ephemeral icons offering certification of our sense of self and self-worth. But there is transcendence in the sense of seeking a communal understanding of what makes us human, each as though her own; our desires as well as our projections, wrapped in each other as they are. Humanity in this sense evokes complacency, whereas inhumanity evokes invention. The inhumanity Apollinaire imagines is not a call to violence but a call to thought and resistance: to resist the power of appearance, the way things look to us in the moment; and to see the light we see by, the light of people, to see illuminate it and further it, and see further.

Perhaps Apollinaire asks too much of himself and everyone else, and perhaps a visionary inhumanity dives all too easily into very real mutual destruction and an environment that allows it. And perhaps Robert Delaunay's paintings in these high-octane years sometimes do drift towards a simple adoration of an exciting new world, its modern trappings and toys. Delaunay began his series of paintings *L'équipe de Cardiff* in 1912, showing rugby players jumping for the ball. Over the next ten years in different versions of the painting he added Paris's Ferris wheel, and an advertising billboard for Astra, the airplane construction company. The Eiffel  Tower, icon of modernity itself, starts to emerge in some of the letters of Delaunay's own name. Imaginative agility is starting to fixate, perhaps, not only on team work and travel but virility, gender bias and egoism. And the painted words throughout the series invite ideas of every sort of communication brought into the frame, every combination of the excluded and the included, and ultimately giving the creator complete control of *his* creation.

A little infantile? But then which one of us can claim adulthood as freedom from fantasy? Sigmund Freud's well-known cotton-reel that he watches a child throw away and continuously pull back shows the resilience we already have as children: the resilience to imagine the most desperate separation and loss, to perform it in play and in that way absorb it. But simultaneously the game shows how much of that resilience is built on performances of return, ownership and ultimately redemption. Whatever

Robert's trajectory, Apollinaire's own Orphism, his own pre-war theory of invention seeks to integrate vision with humility. It's an embrace of life in the name of openness rather than enclosure. But even in Apollinaire's hand what a perilous confusion this is of the known and the unknown, the human with the inhuman in the sense that he imagines it; or progress and ideology; or even the prophetic and the demagogic. And in *Seated Woman*, Apollinaire turns the tables, and shines the light of honesty on the fire he was playing with.

V

In researching and writing *Seated Woman* after his return from the front, Apollinaire seems to chart the collapse of that high wire of invention, ambition and generosity. The novella is another attempt to address reality, another reality, a new reality made from the *in*ability, *not* the capacity to think across borders, to espouse borders, to allow borders to refract each other and people to re-engage with each other. Even before the war Apollinaire knew what was a stake, his expressions of simultaneity seek diversity and not assimilation. His understanding of light and darkness is moral as well as perceptual, and his constant ally is a practice of distance. If art is to illuminate not only *what* we see but what we *could* see, what else but an indirect approach can show that? And how else to avoid simply replacing one point of view with another, equally exclusive one? A simultaneity is needed that resists singular points of view without itself imposing one and coalescing into one; and it's needed now just as much as it was then.

Apollinaire's melancholy also comes to his aid once again, frequently he's in conversation with his shadow, 'son ombre', all the inward parts of himself he never meets and are lost to him, even in the speaking. But they are spoken nonetheless, just as his notion of light and shadow is expressed indirectly, at a distance from itself. He imagines a distant anthropological moment: 'tous les hommes aiment avant tout la lumière. Ils ont inventé le feu', 'all men love light above all: so they invented fire.' Fire and light go together, but they are not the same. Love and invention go together, but they are not the same either. If each were the same as the other, neither would exist, and there would be no invention or any desire.

Here's another. 'Quand l'homme a voulu imiter la marche, il a inventé la roue qui ne ressemble pas à une jambe. Il était surréaliste sans le savoir.' 'When mankind wanted to imitate walking, it invented the wheel which looks nothing like a leg: surrealists without knowing they were.' So: imitate to understand. Invent something with which to imitate, then learn from that imitation that invention transforms life, without any aspiration to transcend it, rather embrace its otherness, live its diversity, without which there is no renewal and only stagnation.

These two little linguistic ballets dance together the dances of distance, elements and people and parts of people all combine, and yet move far enough apart to breathe and move, to allow movement and breath, and the imagination of different times and tongues.

Another sort of ballet appears in his poems combining word and image and collected in the book to which they give its name, *Calligrammes*, published in 1918: poems written calligraphically, or that allude to calligraphy; also to Chinese or Japanese ideograms that communicate meaning visually without reference to sound. These poems are integral to Apollinaire's life in art before the war, the wave of aesthetic and moral confidence he was riding, and by contrast they speak volumes to the new art he seeks in *Seated Woman* after the war for a life in pieces. He'd published an initial little group of these poems in 1914 with the title *Et moi aussi je suis peintre*, *I'm a painter too*, and her refers to it impersonally with nostalgia and wry indulgence in Chapter Two of *Seated Woman*. He transcribes the title into Italian, 'Anch'io son pittore', to invent a little saying that evokes the internationalism of Paris in 1916, suggesting that *everyone* wanted to be a painter, not just our inventive Guillaume, and especially the Futurists!

But it's as though Apollinaire knew from the outset that art depends for its optimism on delving into vulnerability in all its guises. Some of these poems show handwriting translated into print, some use printed words, but they all use words to evoke the outlines or the filled-in shapes of objects, animals, people, icons. Apollinaire called the poems in *Et moi aussi je suis peintre* 'idéogrammes lyriques', 'lyrical ideograms': lyrical, once again. More than a fixated melancholy, more than a determined inwardness, Apollinaire's lyricism thrives on the missed connections of life – missed, re-directed, and re-illuminated: the plurality of life on which new directions depend.

'Lettre-Océan', 'Ocean Letter' is one of these calligraphic poems, and how wonderful to find a poem scattering its words across the page! And as your eye wanders and discovers scraps of conversation, passing comments, ephemera, bits of passion and outrage, anything that might find its way onto postcards or telegrams or into letters written at sea, these scraps all merge without merging into a shape you might recognise..., or might have recognised... – but when? At what moment did we fail to see and now do see again – see what? The Eiffel Tower, what else – lost and found in the fabric of life in that moment. Apollinaire imitates that fabric by re-fashioning it; and his invention displays the Eiffel Tower not just for its message of hope and invention but its performance as an icon, its allure, its spontaneous appeal and suspension of anxiety, especially anxiety about everything coming together, intact again, sealed and invulnerable. As though the love of the moment assured the love of everyone, what fun! What freedom!

But the capacity to walk around with all our faculties and our senses and all their antennae working at once is a feature of life, of human as well as animal survival: it does not need to be invented, and to that exact extent it can serve entrenchment as much as generosity. How to re-shape this tightrope of spontaneity and inducement? Or if not re-shape, then illuminate?

Once again, things that belong together aren't necessarily the same, otherwise their affinity would only stifle them and diversity would be lost. Such is the surrealism that Apollinaire foresees in coining the word in his accompanying pieces to his play *Les Mamelles de Tirésias*, *The Udders of Tiresias*, drafted in 1903 and first performed in 1917; and to the ballet *Parade*, first performed in 1917 as well, choreographed by Léonide Massine with sets by Picasso, music by Erik Satie and a scenario by Jean Cocteau. By not being a leg, Apollinaire's re-invented wheel gives greater understanding of walking and the life of humankind on earth. His little story of legs and wheels create or mime chain upon chain of intermediary and redirected encounters, ends and means, and forms. Signs never seem to meet their maker and instead float on the winds: what form might there be to show the life of forms and signs?

In the print-calligraphy of 'Lettre-Océan', there are not one but two wheels, two sets of concentric circles, each offering recognition in the same style of the iconic Eiffel Tower, made up each time of different memories, incompatible micro-perceptions, random associations... And yet all in the mosaic of a single cultural parameter. Like two eyes making one vision and an agility in the world, the vision is still a limited one: limits beyond the seeing, waiting to be seen, lost in the light we see by.

Free simultaneity of its polemical ambition to colonise modernity, and it loses much of its utopianism, and turns instead towards the purity and the realism to which Apollinaire aspired: an ability to allow the transitions of life to sway like grasses in the wind, and from gatherings of joy to ones of confusion or worse.

For what if the clarion calls to democracy emanating from the Eiffel Tower turned icon are overwhelmed by history, and its hurricanes of destruction and incomprehension? As Freud and many others have discovered, egoism and altruism, open-mindedness and defensiveness breathe the same air, and for Apollinaire, neither is understood without the invention of art. And in his optimism of a life devoted to art he seeks ever new forms to show the diversities of order and adventure, as he calls it; but also order and chaos, or generosity and complacency, or again under-standing and simple indifference. In *Seated Woman* he embarks on another voyage, and under pressure to address human violence he seems to feel a still more urgent need for an art able to integrate the aesthetic and the moral. An art of showing rather than telling its own morality, and the search for social understanding. An art to awaken and even convince. If we wonder now, in 2021, what avant-garde art has achieved or ever had the power to achieve, either in Apollinaire's own generation or the one just after, when he was no longer there, Apollinaire asks those questions himself in the multi-vocal narrative of *Seated Woman*. And he does so with a prescience that comes from both impatience and humility, from his fearless energy, his generosity, and his despair.

VI

What a journey Apollinaire leaves behind, travelling the parallel lines of poetry and prose. Let me make an interim ending, drawing to a close my story of Apollinaire's art up to an into Word War 1. 'Un Fantôme de nués', 'A Phantom in the Skies', is a free verse poem from *Calligrammes*, and I'll conclude the book with it later because of its modulations: from absorption in the past to absorption in the present, and from an art of decay to one of wonder. Which one is where?

Where is the French text found in the English one trying to pay homage to it? Published in 1913, 'Un Fantôme de nués' carries in between its own lines and tonalities the range of practices with had so much ambition riding on them. The vast enterprise of breaking up lines and times and points of view in the hope of merging them all, has ended up where it should, in an enumeration that can't be completed. One thing after another, one scrap of insight after another, perceptions teaming and congealing in configurations that displace others – by the time of this poem, it's all sending us chasing remnants and sparks.

But if kisses can be swallowed by ghosts before ever reaching someone, as Franz Kafka might say, they are also blown to the four winds for anyone to feel. Story-tellers send them on their way. The story-teller in this poem is suspended somewhere between Baudelaire and Rilke, and watches an image of himself and other tellers whose stories have survived to help us bind together: the circus performers with the street for a high-top, the *saltimbanques* whose combined agility and dejection artists of different periods have turned to as a way of suggesting their own situation. The state of their aspirations is carried on the masks and costumes of Harlequin and her companions. But for a performer's aspirations to meet the projections of an audience there has to be the will: an invitation, and a show of its acceptance. And here and now there's transaction rather than transcendence; and there's a community of the moment looking again at what frightens and fascinates, wondering again, in these moments of imagination and solidarity, about making a society, and intuiting an understanding that floats on the air with everything still to be shaped, and shared, and given, even in the losing.

VII

One morning the bell woke us up, and as I opened the door and the snow blew in, a red blur jauntily handed me a package. Still without my glasses on I struggled with the professional wrapping, and suddenly it was clear it was the book I was waiting for and had forgotten about. *La Femme assise* itself, édition originale, 1920. On one of the front pages, all the various categories of this original publication were listed in capital letters in a block: different paper for different groups of subscribers, each category with its own way of numbering the copies, the more exclusive ones using Roman numerals or even letters. The print run was 2000 in all, my copy is number 253 of the 800 in the category 'friends of the original edition'. Before the title page, there's another list in the same capital letters of all Apollinaire's publications in book form, two wide and deep books of poetry, three collections of short stories or prose narratives full of dancing myth and lived reality, an art book with Raoul Dufy giving the ancient and the medieval their modern tones, his 'surrealist' play, his ground-breaking book of art writing. The various contributions of other artists are all noted with each title, Derain,

Dufy, Rouveyre, Picasso. And now this novel, *La Femme assise*. There was no more to add to this posthumous list, and never will there be. He was thirty-eight when he died in the influenza epidemic of 1918–1920. How much more might otherwise have come from his mind and his pen as the century unfolded, from his capacity to find an art for the violence of life, and the love needed to embrace it.

Buying this copy of the book as much as translating it have both been ways of honouring the sweep and the range of Apollinaire's life in art. The second came a long time after the first, which was more of a whim and an afterthought, but when the book arrived the sense of gratitude and responsibility or simple attachment was kindled again, reminding me how attachments live on ephemera as much as psychological inlets. And as the pages slipped through my fingers while I sat on the bed and held the book from a hundred years ago, once again I admired the wit and the multiple filters fluttering by as Apollinaire sets Elvire Goulot on her way; Elvira Swig, as she's known in this book. There she was again, a living phantom made from her times and their passing, the passing of all time into history and legend, and all the ways we read them alone and together. Off she goes. But already by the end of that first chapter, and long after the energy of teeming encounters in travel and sex have turned into little more than abuse, the relation of Elvire Goulot to her lover is bathed in disdain like the light of the harvest moon.

Perhaps it's a disdain that floats sideways like emotion will, covering many emotions and thoughts at once. Perhaps Apollinaire's own star waxes and wanes like that of many artists and public figures, as people's attachments are coloured by public as much as private events. Many towards the end of the World War 1 and since have been perplexed, saddened or shocked by the joy and the energy Apollinaire seems to derive from his time as a soldier, participating in mass destruction, cruelty and indifference. Think of 'Merveille de la guerre', 'The Marvel of War' in *Calligrammes*, published in 1918, whose subtitle in English is 'poems of peace and war 1913–1916'. In that poem the poet Guillaume Apollinaire constructs a 'Guillaume Apollinaire' whose name is launched by the war onto the future for all time, transcending history and any distinction between living and dying, or war and sex either. What a suicidal failure and what a travesty of heroism to relish images and ignore how they manipulate.

The young Surrealists-to-be were perplexed, and Louis Aragon still fresh from the killing fields in Alsace is quick to make the point. At the time he and André Breton were becoming friends and collaborators until their ways finally parted again in 1933 over whether, at the aesthetic level, novel writing can ever simply serve the revolutionary cause, and at the political and historical level whether Stalinist communism ever would. Back in 1918, as well as to Aragon, Apollinaire had introduced Breton to Philippe Soupault, the two authors of the *Manifeste du surréalisme*, *Surrealist Manifesto*, published in 1924; and you remember that Apollinaire had coined the word 'surréalisme' in the preface to his 'drame surréaliste', *Les Mamelles de Tirésias*, first performed in 1917. With Apollinaire and surrealism a story of the image is burgeoning – making images; and the appeal of images. Is the image able to capture the wide unpredictability of life? Or does it rather capture you in nets of control that reach far beyond what you can imagine? Does the imagination drive creativity in any case, or is it a witness to its own coercion and the drive to emulate?

Why translate texts by Apollinaire is a question that arises in response to these anxieties. In letters from the front to Breton in 1918 a young Aragon felt betrayed, it seems, in the moment of Apollinaire's death, as though Apollinaire had left his young avant-gardist admirers with nothing but images of nationalist vainglory. In 1917 when Apollinaire was still alive, an equally young Breton to whom Apollinaire had given so much of time and encouragement wrote a piece where admiration and doubt are very finely balanced. Perhaps Breton is a little too quick to apologise for a 'Guillaume Apollinaire' of his own construction, and to misread his own projections just as Apollinaire might be warning against in 'The Marvel of War'. Perhaps too quick as well to use the title of one of Apollinaire's his own works against him, *L'enchanteur pourrissant*, *The Decaying Enchanter*. Published in 1909, it's a book of fantasy and penetrating allegory, where Apollinaire dramatizes quizzically the mystical and transcendent pretensions of poetry down the ages, as well as the boastfulness of human progress.

And yet without some kind of projection of energy there can be no change and the future will remain an image of the present. 'La grande force est le désir' – Breton quotes these lines from 'Les Collines' in his essay: 'The Hill Tops', a poem that readers would see for the first time in 1916 with the publication of *Calligrammes*, and which Apollinaire composes in a poetic form reaching back to François Villon in the late fifteenth century: eight-syllable lines in groups of five. The rhythm he creates is absorbing, galvanising, unstoppable, unpretentious, humble, ambitious, wrought, fluid, purposeful, vulnerable, prone to depression and loss, courageous in the face of all things passing, embracing, democratic, and, once again, generous. It's a generosity coming from an endless pursuit of realism: for what can we ever know of what we know?

We're in 1916, still in mid-war, the year *The Assassinated Poet* was published as well as *Calligrammes, Poems of Peace and War*, and my account in English of the first and last of the two stories in *The Assassinated Poet* appear in this book alongside *Seated Woman*. Soon Apollinaire will start his research for *Seated Woman*, his new novel, and work on it along with other projects until he died, leaving it all but finished. But throughout his writing life, his affective life and his life as a human being, how many signs are there that in peace as well as war Apollinaire understood that poetry cannot deliver revelation or redemption either, and that even our desire for the new is clothed in our understanding of the past and the many forms that it takes, still to be known. *Alcools*, published before *Calligrammes* in 1912 and containing poems written or worked on from 1903 onwards, opens with the last poem to be written for the book, just before it was published. It offers a dynamic though indeterminate 'Zone' in which airplanes are both loved and mocked for competing with the Holy Spirit, and which ends with the sun rising over the Seine as though its throat has been cut.

The last poem in the book was originally published in 1912 as well, and takes its title 'Vendémiaire' from the first month in the French Revolutionary calendar. It replaced the Gregorian one and was used from 1793 to 1805, and again during the Paris Commune of 1871. It begins on the autumn equinox, and the first month is named after the Occitan word for a grape harvester. On the 13th day of Vendémiaire, the first month in Year 4 of the Republic, 5 October 1795, outside the Église Saint-Roch on rue Saint-Honoré in Paris, the forces of the Republic finally defeated a Royalist Catholic insurrection, thanks largely to the strategic use of artillery by Napoléon Bonaparte, their leader. He was on his way. And Apollinaire's 'Vendémiaire' bends the sounds of the classical alexandrine meter to the echoes of a revolution now distant and so completely opposed to everything French classicism stood for. Apollinaire modulates the cries of sacrifice and ecstasy to the tunes in his head of energy, hubris, the violence of progress and oblivion, despair, and new beginnings. Readers are being exhorted to think the future better in the passing of each moment.

Think also of another 'Guillaume Apollinaire': the words of his name are constructed as the reflection of himself in a mirror in a calligraphy of the printed word. I'm thinking of 'Cœur, Couronne et Miroir', a poem in *Calligrammes*, originally in *Et moi aussi je suis peintre* – 'Heart, Crown and Mirror'. The auras of love, myth and power, enchantments of any and every kind remain under the spell of Narcissism, it seems. How to crack the mirror? Or simply show it?

And think too of this short poem taken from Apollinaire's *Poèmes à Lou*, poems taken from the letters he wrote to Louise de Coligny-Châtillon from the front. It's a correspondence in prose and verse full of love, sex and desire, dark melancholy, exasperation and foreboding; and it overflows with poetic wizardry, invention, and with direct and intimate appeal. It's one of two sets of writing Apollinaire sent to lovers during his time as a soldier, first to Lou the aviator, and then Madeleine Pagès the teacher of literature. He met her in 1915 on the train returning to Nîmes from a furlough spent with Lou; Madeleine was returning to her school in Oran in Algeria. He thought he might marry Madeleine but after the shrapnel lodged in his head he seemed to lose interest in life in that moment. But after his return to Paris his inner pulse seemed to return, and as well as embarking on a range of writing and he met and married Jacqueline Kolb.

She gives the title 'La Jolie Rousse', 'The Lovely Redhead', to the last poem in *Calligrammes*, and her avatar makes floating but decisive appearances in *Seated Woman*. The novel as a whole has a weft of references to furloughs, to Paris before the war and during it, also to other wars, different artists, lovers and friends, places and colours – all signs from the present and the past, fluttering adrift from their real names and real relations, released from the real and all the more real for that: all the more affecting, identifiable, open to embrace, and vulnerable to the loss that scatters across our clothes like the insouciance of the rain.

Here's the poem I have in mind, in a slightly different version from the one that appears now in *Poèmes à Lou*, the one André Rouveyre includes in his 1945 account of life with Apollinaire and which so struck me when I read it in my twenties. In that mémoire as well as this little poem, it's as though circumstance, ephemera and fragile temporality carry in them everything we can know about our inner world and the history that floods it.

L'adieu du cavalier

Ah Dieu ! que la guerre est jolie
Avec ses chants ses longs loisirs
La bague si pâle et polie
Et le cortège des désirs
Adieu ! voici le boute-selle...
Il disparut dans un tournant

Et mourut là-bas tandis qu'elle
Cueillait les fleurs en se damnant

The Horseman's Farewell

My God how pretty is the war
The songs and long moments
The ring so polished and pale
And all our desire on parade
There's the bugle, Farewell
He disappeared at the bend
And died over there as she
Cursed the flowers she picked

I've always found translating rhyming poetry especially troubling, let alone song lyrics. Unsurprisingly I would rather avoid it, as I feel I can learn the most and offer the most from translating texts I have an affinity with, not only their sense of things but in my own sense of what I can bring to them. But avoiding difficulty is often a way of avoiding what can be learnt from it, just as avoidance itself sets off the process of learning different things and how to do them. For me translating just like writing produces ways of offering and re-offering texts to readers as well as myself. Rhyme generates association and releases the dormant, and resides in an individual mind's ear as well as an individual language and its innumerable variants. It's an uneasy combination, but also a working and very familiar combination of the singular and the communal. It belongs somewhere without belonging anywhere. To that extent you might say that rhyme offers indefinite freedom as well as indefinite restriction, and translation of rhyme all the more. But the distinction is a false one, or an artificial one, for do we express ideas or are we expressed by them? Are we contained or containing, and what can we learn about what sticks in the mind and the heart. Reading Apollinaire's last lines and the rhymes and assonances, I can almost hear Pete Seeger's song about flowers long gone and the ever-presence of never understanding.

In French literature, Charles Baudelaire often stands out for the way he hears the echoes and the near endless possibilities of rhyme. Endlessly supervised as well. Its interwoven channels of surprise and internalised convention are not heard, felt or practiced in the same way in different languages, and there's nothing surprising there. It's the entry points that matter to hearing the ways we internalize the language given us, as well as the boundaries between our own language and others. I'm especially drawn to rhythm and drawn in by it, I feel it's at the heart of building connections between different texts and different people. I'm not in a position to step outside the way I hear, or the way my subjectivity is fashioned by my history and our history, and translating allows me to show rather than tell something of that inability. To act as though I can stabilize these relations would feel like betraying whatever I'm able to hear in texts, as well as the process of offering texts to others; or re-offering them. And in the open triangulation of translator, reader and text, faithfulness, rhythm, nurture and inconclusiveness all seem to combine.

VIII

Faithfulness to what, you might ask? It seems to depend on the moment. I certainly want to get things right, like any translator might. I don't want to make any mistakes and above all I don't want to mislead. Avoiding giving the wrong impression is a large part of what drives me as a translator, as a basic mark of respect. Impressions…: who can guide or control them, though? How do they accumulate and what is the labyrinth of their effects? In trying to show rather than aspiring to tell, translation offers me the chance to give shape to the impressions left in me by literary texts and to offer a witness to it.

Seated Woman is a novel about the First World War, about living through the war, about imagining what society is possible after the horrific human devastation in the trenches. A few moments ago I wanted to include 'The Horseman's Farewell' because of its opening line, and the way it seems to celebrate rather than despair at war: 'Ah Dieu ! que la guerre est jolie'. But 'Ah Dieu' gives the same sound in French to 'My God' as it does to 'Farewell' ('Adieu'); I wanted show Apollinaire's own witness to the entanglements joy and despair. In the end that meeting of sounds doesn't figure at all in the English I've written (it never seemed likely that it would, did it…?). I'm not writing this as compensation, simply as a further way of showing how what I hear is offered to you to hear in English; or as a springboard to other echoes in your mind altogether. And here rather than rhyme I've tried to use rhythm and soundplay to mime, accompany, and finally perform the little dance of Apollinaire's poem, and the circulation on parade of desire, manipulation and curse.

Not so much poems as songs appear every now and again in *Seated Woman*, punctuating and highlighting the chaotic sweep of events and memories told in many different voices, all riding on the impulsiveness of the moment, many different kinds of moment from many different times, and all held in a style of their own that Apollinaire maintains and shapes and still allows to blow in the wind. Often these are songs of the moment, which in that very moment express the sounds of the past: sometimes a cultural past and a heritage, for good or ill, sometimes a personal nostalgia, painful or creative.

Towards the end of Chapter One there's a tiny fragment of a song that Apollinaire, in something like the main narrative voice of the moment, puts in to show the need to capture things in types, and model life on what seems to typify it. You'll need to imagine the old can-cans to understand what's both expressive and tired about the Moulin Rouge, he writes; and equally you'll need a song from an earlier period to understand what's at once suggestive and limited about Seurat's post-impressionist attempt to capture its mood. Towards the end of the wild Chapter Four there's another song that comes to the mind of Pamela Monsenergues, Elvira Swig's great-aunt, as she wonders what she's doing in Utah swapping a Mormon utopia that confuses diversity with surveillance and demagoguery, for the dance halls she'd left behind in her beloved Bréda in Paris, draped in its own fantasies of fashionable colonialism, and alive in spontaneous sex and other commerce of all kinds.

Later, in Chapter Seven, there's yet another song, or song-without-music; or song with sound silently prompted. The avatars of Apollinaire and Picasso are becoming more and more detached from the people being evoked, and yet if anything still more reminiscent; or giving still more distressing sketches of what might be in store for them and their world in an imaginary future. A foursome develops and on the way home after a night out the little song they sing is once again coloured in an insouciant orientalism, but testifying as well to a multiculturalism as innocent as a Harlequin suit and still more misguided, with investments in violence and incomprehension raging everywhere. Often songs ride on the memory of them and of other songs as well, and remembering them involves wondering whether anyone else does. Translating them rides on this same tentative and hesitant appeal to a community which it can only fail, perhaps: the language distances are too great, and so are the ones of epoch. In response I've tried to listen to the way rhythm generates meaning – for better or worse; and to allow rhythms to emerge to prompt meanings in English, that overlay with English the dance of meanings in these little French songs. Here sound while creating sense, also prevails over it.

Not quite so in the ways I've written in English for the broad sweep of *Seated Woman* as a whole, in all its tonalities, chapters and evolutions. Like the subject-matter they change widely and wildly with each new beginning, and in English I had to listen, follow, mime, exceed, fashion and re-fashion, push and shove, and follow again. But there's a sweep and a rhythm to the narrative nonetheless, and integral to it is another of its returning punctuation marks: the dance of proper names that extends across the whole piece. Fictional or poetic names, real names, sobriquets, pseudonyms, they all leap from everywhere and recede back into the fabric – of what? What's being named and what's being disguised, and what's being said in this word-mime of names and echoes? Each reader will have their own sense of it, as so will any one translator, whose job is nevertheless still to allow this multi-vocal and multi-dimensionless text to breathe in this other language. Who is Pablo Canouris, as he's called in French? He has blue hands. Is he anyone at all other than a fantasy man and of an artist with blue hands? Why look further, when there's no need to ask a question that probably doesn't matter, and that encourages pinning things down that won't be pinned down, and might even draw away from the layers unfolding in the narrative with hardly any direction home?

The chapters read more like a set of analogies and propositions than anything. Or like fantasies written with a mixture of hilarity, love and horror at what human invention seems capable of. What is a society, what society can we hope for in such times of war and peace, where an appearance of free-floating, world-wide diversity seems to feed off enclosures of deafness proliferating everywhere. The name Pablo Canouris chimes in the mind or it doesn't, or perhaps it will later and in different ways. Pablo Blue might invite some to think of Pablo Picasso who went through a blue and then a pink period before his cubism, and on from there to cascades of different styles, each moulded to moments in history that Apollinaire was never to know. It's hard to imagine closer friends and collaborators than Apollinaire and Picasso, or two artists more closely agreed on the power of the past both to invade and nurture, and the need for new thought, practice and life.

But it's a Pablo re-cast to re-illuminate the flawed man that is Pablo Picasso that emerges from *La Femme assise*. What are we to make of that title, taken in part taken from *Femme assise*, one of Picasso's Cubist portraits? In the novel Pablo with the lovely blue hands seems to know very little of how he sees and reacts, or anything much about his own pressure points. Other than his blue hands readers hear very little about his art and very much about his sexual desires and attitudes, translated without mercy into his impulse to control the diversity of all women, and eventually one of the narrators peeps through the fabric and simply pronounces that Pablo had no love for women and only despised them. How far fiction has carried Apollinaire, his narrative voices, and his experimentation with his experimenter friends turned avatars of experimentation? What hope is there remaining of fragmenting the hold of destructive responses to gender and sex?

The question stretches over the entre narrative, punctuated by many different conflicts between different men and women, and still more moments of hearing and failing to hear combined. To that extent I'm translating a text in which translation often fails, and yet translating still offers hope. What's in a name, what does it carry and when and how should it be translated? Pablo Canouris with the blue hands who rejects polygamy but practices abduction, who professes undying love in daily social interaction but is legalistic in his pervasive jealousy... what name is this, that Apollinaire has come up with? How does it suit or not suit the extravagant comedy of extremes that is the figure being named? Extravagant maybe, but what power comedy has to lay out extremes without comment but rather a shrug and a guffaw, and in the next moment we're left to wonder about what do to at all.

I went up various alleys as I tried to hear what Apollinaire was offering me and how I should offer it to you. Conversation brought me to the name I've found, not unlike the conversations in the narrative itself, and arising from what people's education gives them to hear and not hear at the same time. What has love turned Pablo with the blue hands into, what has he become in the name of love? Pablo Canouris. Apollinaire was someone for whom loving, sexing, writing, reading, researching, wondering and wandering were all one. Messages seem to come to him from everywhere he looks, reads and remembers across the epochs and languages of his own erudition. Pablo Canouris: "canis" is Latin for dog, "οὐρά" (ourā) is Greek for the tail of a dog or a lion: Pablo Dogtail. And the French word for tail is "une queue", which is also the common slang word for penis, prick, dick and many others: Pablo Dogdick, or Pablo Dogsprick, the one more throw-away sarcastic than the other.

And responding to the rhythm of how the meaning of the strange-sounding name might appear over an entire reading, I started to wonder whether the name – a nickname after all – needs to be always the same, Pablo with the blue hands could come out as Pablo Dogsprick just as well as Pablo Dogdick or even Pablo Bluedog. I felt that if I alternated between all of them you would know what I was trying to do, and that for the English-language narrator seemingly to care so little about the accuracy of Pablo's name would put him still further in his place. In any case I thought mobility was once again part and parcel of responding in English to Apollinaire's narrative – acting out the mobility of association he offers and the ability to grasp it; but also the vulnerability of association to deep-seated psychic modelling embedded in all directions, backwards and forwards and from side to side.

What's lost? The knowing interplay of ancient languages, and their distant echoes in the modern. What's gained, hopefully? The rhizomic, pervasive and distressing ways in which the past silently fashions the present. But it can only be left to appear. And in spite of giving in to monolingualism (no combination of languages ancient and modern), maybe Bluedog, Dogdick and Dogsprick all together keep at least some of the chortle. I didn't want anything too witty or clever either. However knowing Apollinaire's wordplay, its point is still only to nod in the direction of Cubist Pablo, and beyond that to remind us admirers of what we still need to do if we're to effect any change in world and mind and the legacies that fashion them.

Perhaps it would have been better to say nothing. Laboriously explaining a joke, and then a translation as well! But there's no putting the genie back in the bottle, and perhaps the choice to show rather than tell that I mentioned before, and that's at the heart of my approach to translating and my writing about art as well, is more a tendency than a choice; and perhaps showing can embrace telling after all in something like this essay, or memoir, or re-narrating. I'd always wanted to do my best to have Apollinaire's novel read with ease and spontaneity, and offering it in my English writing without Apollinaire's French one in parallel is a way to try and achieve that, with no invitation to cross-check one against the other. And it leaves me now with the sense of telling a story of a translation and the desire to write it, a story that has many tentacles beyond enumeration and that stretch back into Apollinaire's writing as well as my response to it, and which once again I'm trying now to show rather than tell, describe or define.

And so what of Apollinaire himself, his own name or pseudonym in the narrative? What a protean and ghostly presence he is in his text, sometimes a concerned observer, sometimes an extra, sometimes an auto-biographical voice, sometimes even the protagonist. As narrator he has no name even when he's present in the first person, such as the in the role of solicitous friend to the supposedly suicidal Bluedog, and his melancholic and fundamentally violent amorous obsessions. Later, as I said just now, the narrator judges him without any indulgence or forgiveness. Or think of another earlier first-person intervention that arises seamlessly when the narrator lies in a hospital bed recovering from his wound, and overhears one side of a phone conversation about dolls and doll-portraits. Speculations follow about how miniatures capture history in the associations through which it's lived and remembered and that voice the muffled sediments of a person.

Third-person narration, biography and autobiography intermingle and separate again throughout; as well as the voices of a creative writer, cultural historian, sketch writer and art critic. This drift is nowhere more moving than in the passage at the end of which this musing on dolls emerges, and which has been a segment of an incomplete autobiography of a writer with no name. As a reader you and I are left to imagine an Apollinaire of our own, saying to us that prose is quicker to produce than verse and that he needs to get on. Perhaps it's an invitation to read quickly, but will associations reveal their secrets and their patterns for all that?

In any case it gives the lead to this chapter, how to read it and how to translate it: a kind of deftness and lightness predominates, and I wanted to let that shape me as I found the words in English, wrapped as I was in the tonalities and constrictions of an educated man of letters a hundred years ago. Or you might say that Apollinaire's prose seems to drift sideways rather than in depth, making patterns seem all the more tantalizing and all the more impossible to grasp. I don't want to do more than leave the whole chapter to your own imagination to wonder over, like the rest of the narrative; but in this moment I'd like to imagine us agreeing it reads like a tapestry of diverse voices, cultures, places to meet and misunderstand, interacting and doing business in friendship and rivalry, a tapestry held together in a mind and given to other minds to hold together in their own ways.

But there's a melancholy as well in the evocation of 1916 Paris, mid-war. A Paris made of freedom of thought and practice and action, spontaneous in its lives, loves, ambitions and visions, but now set against its polar opposite in the trenches. A tapestry in the moment of unravelling and being ripped apart by war and the voracious appetite of history to consume itself, cover its traces, perpetuate itself through the people who make it and live it, always ahead but always lost in a tapestry of their own making, woven in the sounds of others woven within.

Lost as much as highlighted, wandering through this tapestry of his own making there appears an Apollinaire under a pseudonym, flagging the limits of his own understanding, the real Apollinaire's – as though he could know them, or any of us could. The joke of a pseudonym is directed at the person it semi-disguises, but the joke turns back onto naming anything at all, sowing doubt and confusion instead of certainty. The pseudo-Apollinaire sets himself in a mild but consistent opposition to his brother-in-art Cendrars, as I suggested before. Neither evades failure. If Cendrars seems to pontificate rather, not least about fantasies of repopulation as central to rebuilding the status of France post-war, at least he introduces Elvire Goulot, to Otto Mahner, who appears in English as Otto Warning, the fake Ovid's great-uncle who spent his boyhood in Salt Lake City amongst the Mormons. And so the whole sweep of the conversation begins about the mirages of political utopia and sexual liberation. Will either materialise? Will they ever combine?

The noun "die Mahne" in German means "reminder" in English, and the verb "ermahnen" means to admonish, exhort or warn. What is Otto warning of, and will his exhortation even be noticed? Whatever the answer, surely both names need to be translated, I thought, or at least some of them, otherwise I'm giving up on everything before I've even started. "Goulot" is the French noun for the neck of a bottle: plunge right in – Elvira Swig. And she's on her way. Exploited, exploiting, theorizing, making art and dealing in the illusions of art: irreverent, impulsive and intuitive, in many ways she's the central character in this narrative with no centre, wondering what a society without war will look like with the tunes of war still ringing her ears. *The Travels of Elvira Swig.*

And so what about those two brothers-in-arms-and-art? What's in a name, or a pseudonym, and especially a pseudonym for people who themselves have chosen to go by a pseudonym? Blaise Cendrars was born Frédéric-Louis Sauser, and Apollinaire brings him into his fantasy, or is it a parable, first by the name of Waxheimer: the fictional-real man's further German alter-ego, apparently incorrect, moreover, in this saga of war-torn migration: a German sergeant still more or less welcome in La Coupole, Montparnasse meeting place for artists and the arty. I wanted to keep the German character of the name and still to translate it, to try and make sure it lives again in English, rather than leaving it to stultify in a web of

German and French association long gone. Not that I wanted to reproduce or imitate, even if I could, but rather prolong this little game as I heard it. Wax- or "wachsen", German for to grow, didn't in the moment seem all that far away from "wichsen", to masturbate or wank. And according to *Urban Dictionary*, "wink" can mean anything from sleep, to salacious suggestions of female genitalia, to literally anything at all, a random word for anything when the proper word can't be found. So: Winkheimer; pronounced with the English "w" or the German one sounding like an English "v" – as you like. (Does anyone remember Carol Reed's film *The Third Man?*) Wankheimer would have been too obvious in any case, not that this play with names is overly subtle, nor is any of them in this novel; they seem both obvious and obscure, rather like the causes of war.

You remember that the reason why anyone would think this character is Cendrars at all is through the fictional swapping of wounds that Apollinaire fashions: it was Cendrars who lost his arm and Apollinaire who came home with a wound to the head, rather than a head-wound for Cendrars and wounded arm of Apollinaire as in the story. Mobility or confusion? And when will that confusion itself come to an end? This character's other pseudonym in the narrative, you remember, is Ovide du Pont-Euxin, the name under which he enlisted in the Foreign Legion. Ovid – the Latin poet of transformation: transformation controlled by powers we wonder at, and ultimately fail to understand: how appropriate to wartime. The Euxine Sea is the Black Sea in Ancient Greek. Arrian of Nicomedia, best known as a historian of the campaigns of Alexander the Great, champion of "civilization" by colonization and plunder, also wrote a periplus (Latin for an itinerary of ports) of the Euxine Sea.

Is Cendrars being slipped in as kind of geographer, map-compiler, taxonomist of the modern? With little understanding of its spirit, energy, and vitality – or its violence either?

Or is the invitation in Ovide du Pont-Euxin to think of Ovid's *Tristia ex Ponto* and his *Epistulae ex Ponto*, elegiac couplets and letters he wrote in Pontus on the Black Sea, now Constanta in Romania, where he was in exile from Rome 8 a.d. until his death in 17 or 18 a.d.?

In any case the narrator in whatever voice frequently calls him the fake Ovid, a fake poet with no real intuition of what governs his times, and whose lamentations and diagnoses seem merely to finger-wag and confirm his exile.

As to the rest of this pseudonym, Pont-Euxin reminded me of aristocratic names, also Bordeaux wines such as the Pomerol Château Pont de Guîtres. In my ear that harmonic drew me to including St in the name as it travelled in English: Ovid St Euxine; which moreover reproduces the mixture of the pagan and the Christian suspended over the whole novel.

A certain pomposity, a certain fakery, a certain pretention and dandy-ism, even a certain amateurism is projected by Cendrars' pseudo-nym: will Apollinaire's pseudonym fare any better? Anatole de Saintariste. It's separate from the general third-person narrative voice, as well as the first-person one that occasionally appears. It includes saints and sainthood, *Saint*ariste, and in this English incarnation of the novel the Saints have swapped bodies like the same two have swapped wounds – the Saint of Saintariste has gone over the St Euxine. And so the two continue, each to his own, their ballet of reserve and suspicion: more inward in the melancholic Apollinaire, however exuberant, than in Cendrars, with his more consistent self-belief. Saintariste appears for the first time in the same crowded scene at La Coupole as the fake Ovid does, and here's the first broad hint that Saintariste might be part of Apollinaire's wardrobe of alter ego's. Saintariste is recovering from his fictitious wound to the arm, he's on his first outing to the café with his new companion, the lovely Coralie with the red hair, who taken as a whole looks like a drop of blood on the blade of a sword.

'La Jolie Rousse', 'The Lovely Redhead', is a real part of the life of the real Apollinaire: Jacqueline Kolb, who had red hair and whom he married after his return from the fighting. Her avatar appears with a pseudonym of her own in *La Femme assise*, but gives rise to thoughts of inconstancy rather than fidelity. 'La Jolie Rousse' is also the title of the last poem in *Calligrammes*, a book published in 1916 you remember, and the poem seems written in an explosion of fervour, optimism, and belief in the power of art to set mind and body free. The voice in the poem seems unable see past its own limits and instead fashions a manifesto in its own image, a devotion to "l'Ordre et l'Aventure", "Order and Adventure", the need to hear the voices of history with clarity, and to fly with them towards untold visions and new relations. Order and adventure, simplicity and the multifaceted need each other to fly, like Apollinaire's fictional though still legendary birds from China, who have a single wing and fly in pairs.

They appear twice, once in 'Zone', the opening poem of *Alcools* and the last in the book to be written, in 1912; and later in *Calligrammes*, in "Les Fenêtres" which I talked about before, and which was written just a few months later in 1913. There's been a poetic drama in that short interval: the magical birds with one wing that need each other to fly have been reduced to nothing but their giblets. And beyond *Calligrammes*, this book of poems of 'peace and war', what a battering the dream of integrating tradition and invention will have taken in the life and mind of Apollinaire, as he researched and composed *Seated Woman*.

> Laugh and laugh as much as you like
> Peoples of everywhere and especially here
> How many are the things I've not dared say
> So many things you've not let me say
> Mercy, mercy, pour mercy on us all

> Mais riez riez de moi
> Hommes de partout surtout gens d'ici
> Car il y a tant de choses que je n'ose vous dire
> Tant de choses que vous ne me laisseriez pas dire
> Ayez pitié de moi

In another plea for mercy like this one at the end of 'La Jolie Rousse', and at the very end of *Calligrammes*, I hope you'll forgive me for changing 'me' to 'us', and modulating so much else besides as I try and serve what Apollinaire is giving me to hear, about his time and its passage to ours; about what we can know and not know, say and not say; and about each one of us shows and knows about the love and hate of our times, and still fails to tell.

The lovely Coralie of *Seated Woman*, who's named after the red-coloured stone and is like a drop of blood on a sword and is, accompanies Apollinaire's avatar in a defining moment or two for him – the fictional Apollinaire, through whom the real one is trying to show the pressures of being at war and returning from war. You'll remember the final outcome at this point, and the way it's emotionally anticipated, so to speak, as the two wander home one night and Coralie tells him of her unfaithfulness to Hyacinthe Brionne, his friend and her former lover before he was killed.

Once again, what's in a name? Hyacinth Brionne. The beautiful Spartan Hyacinth was the lover of Apollo, god of the arts of mind and body, whose echo is carried in the pseudonym Apollinaire. The god of the west wind Zephyrus also loved him, and the god of the north wind Boreas too, as well as the man Thamyrus, the singer from Thrace, the country of Orpheus now absorbed jointly in Greece, Turkey and Bulgaria – battle grounds all in World War 1. Hyacinth was killed by accident in a manly game of quoits with his chosen lover, the god Apollo  – or did Zephyrus intervene, the jealous west wind, blowing Apollo's quoit off course and killing the one who'd spurned him? Apollo couldn't join his human lover in death, he planted his lament on earth in the flower he named after him, the sound of which, in Ovid's words, mimics the sound of despair – *ai, ai.*

Henri de Lorraine, Comte de Brionne was a military aristocrat at the court of Louis XIV, and over the vast spaces of the millennia from Antiquity to Neo-Classical France, heroism has transformed step by glory-inspired step into pageantry. The engraver Jacques Callot illustrated *Le Combat à la barrière, The Combat at the Barrier,* a book by Henri Humbert published in 1627 and devoted to a lavish tournament organised by the then Duc de Lorraine. Close by you'll see an allusion to the first of Callot's etchings, it evokes rather soberly the immense grandeur and

 the equally meticulous detail involved in the event. But what further artistry is devoted in the other etchings to presenting participants in a mythological, human-animal guises, and fantastical allusions all loaded with extravagant pretention and claims to omnipotence.

Hyacinth Brionne: Eros and Thanatos, life and death, love and forbidden love, pomp and circumstance, blood and suffering, glory and legend. Who can disentangle them? Or service from self-aggrandisement; or altruism from egoism? And sacrifice from vast carelessness and waste?

Anatole de Saintariste, home wounded from the front and in love with the lovely Coralie who's like a drop of blood on the blade of a sword, is the name-disguise of Apollinaire. He has a wound in the arm instead of the head, and late in the narrative Apollinaire begins to wrap him in a dwindling taste for the Paris and its artists of before the war, which another Apollinaire-voice drew so much energy from earlier in the narrative, however nostalgically. Saintariste is devastated by emotional betrayal, which spreads sideways as the lovely Coralie leaves him, as she had Hyacinth, this time for Elvira and a different life. His sense of personal futility spreads to a generalised one, and he looks back upon his times with an astonishment that drifts into horror. What has it all been for, all this destruction and killing, and what can he do now? He theorises and comes up with the last great societal theory of the novel, an ex-soldier-on-the-scrap-heap theory: a religion without dogma and without priests, and whose vocation is the moral and physical education of children. Saintariste as a name is made up from the Christian and the pagan. First of all a saint; and then the Ancient Greek word "agathos" which means "good" in English, in the most general sense. Its superlative, "best", is "aristos"; and Anatole de Saintariste seemed to find a good home in Anatole Holybest – a bit less obscure in the sense of monolingual, in the same way that Canouris went from a French-sounding word made of Latin plus Greek to an English-sounding one made of English plus English: Bluedog or any one of the others. But how obscure was Apollinaire's French bilingual portmanteau anyway? Never too obscure to stifle the satire of his little inventions, or the wryness, or finally the hopelessness.

The Saint in the French made-up name Saintariste is lost in Holybest; but Ovid St-Euxine has acquired it. And the other way around: the fake Ovid in English has acquired a Saint in St Euxine, which also speaks to the mockingly aristocratic-sounding Pont-Euxin in French, which itself echoes the "aristo" buried in Saint*ariste*. One name bleeds into the other as each travels between the two languages. And in the end it's Ovid St Euxine with whom Anatole Holybest shares his own version of utopia and his last-ditch pursuit of honour. For it appears only honour can safeguard education, authenticity and respect against weaponised dogma. Dream on.

Where St Euxine remains on safe territory with stats and systems for repopulation, the aspiration of Holybest was always to elevate and edify. Now he wants to found a religion with no priests but only the only voices of honour: Holybest; a religion or an art for the best, and that leads to the best, with prophets as leaders. Holybest, Apollinaire Holybest, who now seeks prophets of what's already in the fibres of people and nations: collectivity and openness to other nations. His new religion and his new society germinate from tradition, but also from the power to shed tradition like buds emerging from leaves. It develops in opposition to the Mormonism modulated in the feminine of Elvira Swig. And this starkly false choice signals the distance travelled from the easy, though still tense fluidity of mind and mores in Paris before the war and during the early years of the war: you remember that Apollinaire-the-narrator, the one hidden but present everywhere, evokes this period towards the beginning of the story with the deftness of the sketch artist, the intuition of the creative historian, and the poet's feel for the power and constraint of associative networks. The religion without dogma and the Mormonism in the feminine both exceed the pedantic dandyism of St Euxine, Holybest's interlocutor on social theory in his final days. But only one of the two imaginary societies survives.

Drawn at the end to St Euxine with whom he seemed to have no natural affinity, or even much contact at all, Holybest is killed in a tangle with Moses Ladder. At the other end of the story, right at the beginning, Apollinaire had introduced Moses Ladder by writing that he's far more interested in him than most others, and would far rather tell us about him than the son of Leopold von Sacher-Masoch, of whom in fact we hear very little indeed. This is Apollinaire the narrator again, still in disguise, then, but dropping his guard as he does sometimes, and speaking in the first person; and yet in the first person or not, what voice is there without disguise or clothing? To bear further witness to this, the Apollinaire showing signs of himself in every nook and cranny of the narrative seems welded to accuracy and realism in amongst the profusion of legend. What legend is there in any case but the ones incubating in the materiality of life and history? The historical Apollinaire knew and helped the son of historical Sacher-Masoch, Sir Egon Allemannic, another translated pseudonym for someone with the singular vice of feeling constantly under threat of court action for his particular sexual pathology. But the historical Apollinaire gliding in amongst the textual avatars that grow out of himself claims to prefer the exquisitely marvellous Moses Ladder. Claim as much as you like, how can this juxtaposition be disentangled?

In the end Sir Egon Allemannic simply fades away, and as soon as Moses Ladder appears it was clear to me that this was another name that needed to be translated. You remember he makes music with different parts of his body, his stomach turns into the sound-box of a cello and with his feet he makes the sound of a rattle snake – connected I'm sure to the sound like parchment of the dresses worn by the fifteen wives of the Elder Perciman that we hear about later. The one sound is linked to the other along shreds of verbal patterns that are either picked up or not, and with a meaning that may or may not appear. The name in French of Moses Ladder is Moïse Delechelle, Moses Oftheladder, and it's no leap at all to go from a ladder with the forename Moses the Biblical figure of Jacob, and from there back again to the Parisian avant-garde with Apollinaire reaching out to Max Jacob, for whom Moses Ladder is as thin a disguise as Moïse Delechelle. Or at least I hope so. I felt the name needed to be translated to have any life in English at all, but also that even though I'm doing so now, the translation needed to avoid drawing too much attention to itself. After all the joke really isn't that funny, it's just a joke.

Initially, at least. And a joke on whom, anyway? The real Apollinaire had caught a hold of the pastiche and the satire of Jacob's writing, which grew increasingly biting, increasingly desperate at its own failure to dent the power of legend, and myth, and the indefinite cultural shaping of the mind. French to the core of his identity, persecuted by the Nazis in the next war for being a Jew despite also being a Catholic, Jacob was arrested in St Benoît in Brittany in interned in Drancy where he was ultimately murdered in 1944. And at the end of this story which looks backwards and inwards at devastation, and forwards to any hope at all of re-building and re-stitching society, Anatole Holybest and Moses Ladder end up blown to pieces together. The lost idealist and the lost artist: what a mess.

Each in his own way might represent Apollinaire himself, the real blood-and-bones artist: on the one hand, the soldier dedicated to an idea of France that embraces collectivism and openness; on the other, the writer famously accused of being nothing much more than a junk shop owner, making so-called art out by assembling bits of ephemera and detritus. I'm sure Apollinaire could live with that taunt, despite the frustration and the pain; and also with the real conflict in himself between thoughts of solidarity and fragmentation. But what if that were just my imagination, what if he weren't able to live with the taunts and the conflict, and what if he weren't incorporating conflict but blown apart by it? What if the very attempt to rise above the contradictions of history is a further sign of their powers? Lying in the same pool of blood and locked in an embrace, here's Anatole Holybest, a pawn whose generosity and melancholy are putty in the hands of a self-interested, self-promoting and destructive nationalism; and here's Moses Ladder, the object of anti-semitic suspicion even from Holybest, a Moses Ladder now lost in his own marginalisation and fear, and his increasingly fraught involvement with the market in wartime memorabilia and shells. War, art and trade, freedom, suspicion – who can disentangle them? And what a mess of fear, resentment and despair at the near-end of *Seated Woman*.

IX

What's in a name? Or in inventing one, and translating an invention? With Cubism and Orphism Apollinaire sailed the wide open seas of Eros, the collapse of borders and the free movement of thought and light. Now Thanatos has taken the wheel in these stories of war, borders are no sooner crossed than multiply, and no formalist fragmentation can ever strip individual perspectives of what they are – a multi-dimensional network of fortifications and guises, just like the encounter made of writer, translator and reader, with the invitation to pass through all the more urgent. But to where?

You may remember a moment early on in *Seated Woman* where the narrator, this time in his guise of an autobiographer with no name, evokes words passing out of use, but being planted in their texts by later writers to give a flavour of the past. It's mobile moment in the time of the narrative, where that intermittent voice with no name or place either contemplates the passing of all voice and name. It's also a moment of understated satire on the poetry of Paul Verlaine and his book *Fêtes Galantes* of 1869, where by the smoke and mirrors of poetry-making, melancholy provides a fixed point from which to control a fixed past – a nostalgic idea of "the eighteenth century" – with its own stagnant words and fixated images. The melancholy of Apollinaire's voice with no name is of a different kind, it contemplates its own disappearance along with the names he loves and the voices that carry them. To dissolve perspective is to dissolve attachment, and yet without attachment the past cannot be told from the present which is its only domain. Such is Apollinaire's journey from *Les Peintres cubistes* with no thought of war on any horizon, to *La Femme assise* just at the end of World War I. Fragment to explore and re-discover has veered into the fragmentation of any aesthetic, moral or social purpose.

How to translate the flavours of the past carried in names, when names in a different language carry different flavours and a different past? Occasionally I left them in French, but often a name in French in an English text just sounded distant and deprived of any resonance. Names of the *bals musettes* spring to mind, as well as cafés: I felt caught between trying to resuscitate the sound-associations of the French names in my ears, and trying to make sounds-associations in my English ears that make their own way. I'm also thinking of the names of the can-can and other performers at the Moulin Rouge, all made well known by the paintings of Georges Seurat and Henri de Toulouse-Lautrec, both mentioned by the over-arching narrative voice with no name.

Performers well-known to some, perhaps; but familiarity passes with time. So I translated some of these wonderful stage names, preserving some-times quite literally whatever mystery or bizarreness I could: The Glutton – La Goulue; The Ray of Gold – Rayon d'Or; Gutter-Grate – Grille d'Égout; Vincent the Boneless – Valentin le Désossé (issues of rhythm for me, there). On the other hand, and turning to the bals musettes, less literally le bal de la Jeunesse became Juventus. In times of high brand exploitation, I suddenly felt a connection between then and now, and a heightened sense of how sport, fashion and attraction continue their historic dances on top of the volcanos of destruction, with avoidable and unavoidable death beating from the same civilised heart.

I'm struck again by the thought that it would have been better to say nothing. One of the pleasures, in addition to an act of love, involved in translation is letting the original text speak for itself through the translated one. What an illusion. But just a moment. Critical writing can aspire to make offerings that address the distances between an artwork and the person making it, a person making a text in response, and a reader. And translation can offer its own awareness of those distances by remaining silent, and allowing them to breathe and do their work. I'm not thinking of a self-effacing sort of silence, nor is the translated text any sort of gatekeeper. Instead by remaining silent in plain sight, literary translation can show, or perhaps mimes the unfurling of another text now buried in itself. Through the difference between languages, for me translation signals the pulse of association, illumination, also blindness, but also hope. I think of it as a craft in the silent.

Even so, a text in translation speaks loudly; and yet as a translator I would still far rather stay silent. Or in any case I'm drawn into saying something about translation along different paths from, say, Percy Shelley, Charles Baudelaire, Walter Benjamin, Anne Carson, Clive Scott, to mention just some of the creative thinkers and practitioners who have opened my mind and whom I love to read. What can I take responsibility for, in staying silent? Or trying to stay silent, but still writing these pages? There is no doubting the indirect effects of writing anything, whether a translation or an essay. But in a long moment of war between those who love cultural fortifications and those who love the diversity of cultures, I was drawn with a slow-burning magnetism to *La Femme assise* and to writing *Seated Woman*. What can I say now about the offering I'm making, or would it once again have been better to say nothing?

I started with the need to tell a story about how Apollinaire might have travelled from the adventurous optimism of his avant-garde poetics, to the equally adventurous pessimism of this short novel that travels so seamlessly between hilarity and despair. I wanted also to say something about why I felt that shift would be best communicated by writing a translation. With the understanding belonging only to a true revolutionary of the mind, Benjamin imagines translation having still greater effect on the world than the original text, for now the original text is dissolved into feelers extending indefinitely into all the languages of the world, drawing on them and enlarging them at once. A poetic account of translation if ever there was one – of the poetry of literary translation and the poetry required of it. I'm not thinking of the aspiration to be a poet, but the need for a literary translator to invent a poet so as to think like one. Nor am I thinking of inventing Apollinaire or re-inventing him. Having translated Plato's *Symposium* into English in 1818, in *A Defence of Poetry* of 1821 Shelley writes about poetry and love together. Love is

> a going out of our own nature, and an identification of ourselves with the beautiful which exists in thought, action or person, not our own. A man to be greatly good, must imagine intensely and comprehensively; he must put himself in the place of another and of many others; the pains and pleasures of his species must become his own.

At hundred years' distance, and across the distances of language and idiom as well, Shelley's ambition and simplicity sound like the ambition for society riding on Apollinaire's pre-World War 1 art of simultaneity, its explosion and inclusivity of voice. But a hundred years on again, and looking back at Apollinaire's own journey through love and art right up to his death in the 1918 flu epidemic, two days before Armistice Day, what if transporting yourself and into the voice of others involved voices of confusion and resentment, fear and anger, fakery, inauthenticity and exploitation? And what if the desire to join hands with all others were limited to the moment, to the idea of others surfacing in the moment and allowed by its politics? What if Apollinaire's aesthetically-fashioned idea of generosity had reached that point of endless dispersal and loss?

So if I want to be a quiet translator it's only partly because I would like you to read Apollinaire's novel without interference: and once again, isn't in my power as a translator, a writer, a friend, a partner, a scholar, a teacher or anything else to remove interference from your readings or mine. It's more that I would like to mime the silence at the heart of Apollinaire's own very noisy text. Translators are often compared to Hermes, the mythological messenger of the gods of antiquity. Currently perhaps we have a tendency to herd messengers into one or other of two categories, the good or the bad, and a tendency either to fete our messengers or shoot them. But what a wondrous rather than subaltern position Hermes occupies in the culture of antiquity, not so much delivering messages from the gods but simply the message that gods live among people and people with their gods, their projections, fears, aspirations and ambitions, as much hubristic as creative. Hermes is a messenger of diversity itself, without which neither gods nor people have any air to breathe or invention to drive them.

So to offer a silent translation without interference is only a way of saying something about interference and noise in translation. And the legends through which reality is read live there too. Anne Carson's book *Nox* is a series of dances in with the veils of grief, which she connects to translation as well as history. Writing about Herodotus, the supposedly original historian, she admires his capacity to hear history in the questions people ask of the past and what they resort to in seeking answers. This ranges indeterminately from event to myth, and is both condensed and dispersed in the phrase she translates with the common French saying "on dit", people say. Apollinaire's own way, among so many other writers, of responding in *La Femme assise* to the extravagance of what people say or suppress is something I wanted silently to show in *Seated Woman*.

People say, record or invent all sorts of things in trying to make sense of the world, or laugh at it, or dominate it, and to profess silence in translating what's said is a way of trying to remain open to it. In thinking about translation and translators I'm frequently drawn to Margaret Jull Costa and her translations into English of José Saramago in particular which I'm opening again now. Also the English translations of Michael Hulse and the later ones by Anthea Bell of W G Sebald. Or again the translations into French of Cees Nooteboom by Philippe Noble. In each case what overwhelms me and fills me with the desire to translate is the effect of rhythm. Rhythm in words is full of sound and yet wordless. Rhythm cannot be adapted or recreated in another language, only rediscovered there by individuals in the loose company of others. In rhythm there's memory, association, loss – even what's lost in seeing and hearing.

Thinking of writing history as a struggle with oblivion, Anne Carson wonders what the smell of nothing might be like, and I imagine that the smell of nothing is like what I'm trying to translate: not the fear of a void, but all the pressures close up and dispersed everywhere through which what is heard is both heard and not heard. Perhaps it's found between the wings of Apollinaire's bird that I mentioned before, the bird with a single wing that *remains single* and *still* needs the other wing to fly, now with the smell of nothing between them. It's an in-between distance made from, and also limited by the voices each one of us is given to hear. And rhythm is their domain. Rhythm is everything when it's time silently to show not tell.

Its pressure points are active in the detail as well as the broad sweep of the narrative. I've said something, far too much, about the translation of names, when to translate and when not, what matters and what matters less, how the appearance of names and their translation affects the invitation to read on, and how it punctuates the rhythm of reading, its flow and its interruptions, some rude, some welcome. A moment ago I mentioned how in one of his narrative voices, Apollinaire rues the temptation to include words that supposedly give a bit of local colour or sense of period. How they stick out and distract… But as a translator I run the risk of doing the same. How to translate a word gone out fashion, and alluring for that reason? How to translate a word going out of use into one going out of use in a different language, where it's never existed except in supposed equivalents, each of which will all have its own flow of echoes? It's the rhythm that needs to be not so much captured as let loose, the rhythm of echo and disappearance. And now a hall of mirrors opens up in which one language refuses to be located in the other, and yet still any language is entangled in others. To worry about how one language risks appropriating the other it translates, colonising it with fake familiarity, is only the beginning. The lost sound of a word in the past still resonates falsely and loudly, just as the passage of disappearance itself resonates across languages without being tracked. Translation begins in such moments for me, and perhaps readers and translators can imagine each other across an intersection of languages, in the rhythm of words in sentences and thoughts in flow.

X

Sometimes flow can deceive, and many have wondered about the ways translation can be too good for its own good; too seamless; too enamoured of its own smoke and mirrors; and too ready to prolong the projections and attachments that it hosts. But already it feels like shadow-boxing with ghosts, and I'm reminded of Bertolt Brecht's attempts to break the spells of identification which alert viewers still further to their ideological and affective power. But disruption does exist in the moment, and I leave it to you to decide whether the occasional excursions in *Seated Woman* into contemporary unofficial idiom signal anything other than the pleasure of it; jernt for 'bistrot', for example. In any case they are further attempts to enact the passing of words and their ability to strike wanted, as much as unwanted chords.

What words does Apollinaire use to indicate race, nationality, sex and their proliferating stereotypes? They are at the heart of his enterprise in *La Femme assise*. What society of nations can there be after the industrial slaughter of World War I? Writing *Seated Woman* was an opportunity for me to show and not simply describe how Apollinaire's question resonates a hundred years later, in a further, seemingly endless collapse-and-rebuild of the empires of capitalism and nostalgia. I felt that offering these resonances in translation would allow them to breathe, and the vulnerability as well of what have to say, and also how easily it can go unheard. The novel starts as you remember with that free-floating voice musing about cultural mobility in Paris even up to the last year of the war, and all the people, performers, places, place-names, businesses, brands and banners involved; and all these bits prompted the question translate or not translate, with the desired effect always being to resuscitate them just enough to send them along. For what can be heard in the moment and the confusion of lived history?

Which is the foreground and which the background? What began as an avant-garde experiment, a practice and an artistic revolution of hope has arrived at a place of chaos and destruction. Cubist and simultaneist art of all kinds promised indefinite reconstruction of the world, access to the world and access of people to each other. It promised a formal explosion of disparate elements and moments that would create new context in the moment, a fusion that would bind people engaging with art together, and allow history to be opened up once more to its optimism. But the enterprise was never without melancholia, broken attachments produce as much vulnerability as strength, and society is entangled once more in generosity and betrayal. Words of nation and race are everywhere in Apollinaire's nostalgic but awe-inspiring evocation of cultural fluidity at the start of *Seated Woman*. But it quickly spills into sex trafficking and abduction in the guises of freedom of movement, thought and desire.

This stream of confusion is carried along on those words of race and nation which signal not only diversity, but an evolving, ever re-emerging entrenchment. In translating them I wanted to tread that line without sanitising or excusing. Perhaps once again it would have been better to say nothing, but to do so would be to say nothing about my choices; then again, to say nothing might address the overestimation of the power of choice. I wanted *Seated Woman* to express the anxiety I heard in *La Femme assise*, its vision of cultural, sexual and political relation hardening into deaf-mute incomprehension and resentment. It already has. Does Apollinaire see past this, and what is his vision of renewed society, of any society after such committed destruction in Europe at war? I don't know how far he sees, or how far I can see to meet him either. But I wanted the words of race, sex and nation in the narrative, and the visceral attitudes they carry to show something of all the enclosures and prisons entangled in the sounds of our understanding.

For the past is always present, and the dolls, portraits and models that ultimately charm that nameless narrator at the beginning, by the end have wrapped Holybest, Apollinaire's avatar, in a mist he can't dispel. Nostalgic attempts to recapture, perhaps even re-direct the charisma of the past proliferate in the narrative in ways that still dazzle me, they speak in many tongues and tomes and rhythms, each of which demanded a response from me, and reminding me of Apollinaire's own way of using literature to tell the stories of history. That flimsy, seductive freedom of thought, association and conversation evoked at the start of *La Femme assise* is carried along throughout on the wonders of the stereotype.

In those early moments of the novel the voice of the narrator is dispersed everywhere before settling on the wounded soldier recovering in hospital; and the narrator evokes the many wonders of the stereotype by saying he doesn't see that one, all-inclusive, mobile and volatile stereotype of his own times. If there's one at all it's dispersed everywhere, like that narrative voice itself, entangled in the rush to keep up with the moment and wrapped in the rhythms of insouciance and melancholy. A rhythm for caring and not caring at once, or for melancholy at not caring anymore; or just a floating rhythm for loss and energy combined. Lost identifications follow lost understanding, with the return of the iron-fisted point of view hot on their heels time after time.

I've tried to give life in English to Apollinaire's many abrupt changes of rhythm and tonality and the perceptions that ride on them. That range is still contained within the elastic panorama of stereotypes and the loose community of perspectives known as a context. I felt my job was to promote surprise and disruption, while at the same time picking up the threads of continuity and running silently through them. This range of perspective and rhythm spans both form and content, and it's the tangle of experience, thought and style that Apollinaire tangos with – a coherent tangle which involves numerous changes of narrator and point of view.

Take as an example the leap from that nostalgic evocation of freedom of art and conversation in Paris, to the grotesque black humour later in the narrative of families and lovers separated by enmity and conjoined in infidelity, all to the chamber music of competing artillery fire. It's a gun-music, told from a point of view that's initially unstated and dispersed; and it reminds me of the competing rhythms of *Le Sacre du printemps*, *The Rite of Spring* by Igor Stravinsky, with Vaslav Nijinsky in the wings on the opening night furiously beating out the coherence-refuting rhythms for the dancers to obey. There was scandal at the Théâtre des Champs-Élysées on 29 May 1913, and it is it too much to imagine Apollinaire satirising one scandal-turned-pantomime with another, a purely aesthetic despair with the very physical one of limbs flying about, in one of innumerable such scenes of war in eastern Europe?

There, the tone of grotesque, but also hilarious irony is explicit. But what about the completely different tone in litigious account of the painter-turned-stalker Pablo Bluedog, and his aggressive separation from Elvira Swig? The whole neighbourhood takes sides, whether they know any of the reality or not. A moment of celeb culture out of control? Not to mention the attempted revenge porn? In the end a deal is arrived at, although it doesn't last long as Elvira continues to waver between Pablo and Nicolas, which doesn't last long either. But if this is a moment of eery cultural prescience, now think of Holybest's vision of The Nine Worthies from the past, the mythic embodiment of medieval chivalry – three pagan, three Jewish, three Christian. It arises out of Holybest's sadness and panic listening to his Coralie, his partner since returning from the front, telling him about her infidelity to his friend Hyacinth Brionne, the stretcher-bearer with the redolent name, while he was at the front himself. Is there any honour in war, and is there any way to remove the impulse in men to war, destruction and dominance at all costs? The question begins more and more insidiously to obsess Holybest, as he tries in vain to come to terms with life after the front. And it's one of Apollinaire's own overwhelming thoughts as well as he composes *Seated Woman*, returning to past research and drafts.

Hardly any chapter in the narrative is the same in tone and rhythm as any other, there's much for the reader and translator to catch up with, latch onto, and hear or not hear. For juxtaposition, where things appear in a row, easily drifts into superimposition where one layer covers the others and silences them. There's a conflict of impulses in the novel between generosity and the insatiable desire to control or kill, and it's been my task as a translator to respond in rhythm as much as content to what can and cannot be learnt from history, the one entangled in the other in the confusion of the moment.

XI

Think of how Brother John Taylor and Otto Warning tell the story of Mormon society and a Mormon sense of entitlement. One is bourgeois, and entirely immersed in Mormon ideology; the other working-class, self-educated, erudite, alert. Each with a story-telling power and style shaped by their character. Writing while World War 1 was still raging, Apollinaire imagines a proselytizing trip for Brother John Taylor from Utah to Europe and Paris at the time of the 1848 Revolution, the collapse of the Second Republic and the establishment of the Second Empire in 1852. The letter Apollinaire gives him to write to his Leader and Mormon Prophet about his experiences is wrapped in the tone of an innocent abroad from the century previous toApollinaire's own and his readers'. Its style has the mind-set of a traveller marching straight into his own projections rather than a society at all different from his own.

French nineteenth-century cultural and revolutionary history is strikingly evoked nonetheless, told, re-told, re-cast and re-fashioned with all the telling detail that might so easily convince, with even some idiom of the period. Think of Taylor's account of the barricades arising from the Coup d'État of 1851. Patriotism and fantasies of national utopia float about everywhere, and in Apollinaire's writing ideological, commercial, sexual and racial oppression all speak the language of altruism and democracy. I felt the tone of an educated-ignorant, teacher-student-propagandist carrying me along in an extraordinary weave of travel and psychic immobility. And then come the reminiscences of Otto Warning, his Mormon childhood unfurling like a technicolored ribbon woven in observation, response and story-telling: it's the voice of a particular person and also of any person fashioned by their life-context – a jitterbug of judgement and affect; also extravagance and insouciance. Tone, rhythm and perspective combine differently in each of these narratives, and differently all over the novel as well. The diversity of narrative voices *from* the past and *addressing* the past together show the kaleidoscopic influences that shape cultural understanding, also prejudice; openness as much as exploitation, and progress as much as enslavement.

What a mess of shaping and being shaped. Think of the self-aggrandising illusion of John Taylor and others that patriarchal polygamy liberates people from patriarchal monogamy. In Sigmund Freud's civilisation of discontent, the traumatic effects of organising family, society, and nation all from the position of the father are as multiple as the ways invented to counter them. And in the times evoked across the pages of *Seated Woman*, cultural diversity is ever vulnerable to fear, resentment and arrogance, and veers alarmingly into self-regard and aggression. Will inclusion ever be immune to assimilation and coercion? And think now of the conversation in Salt Lake City between the Ute Chief Milopitz and the Jewish trader Chéri de Mendoza, as they stand and watch the lavish Mormon parade go by in which neither is involved. Myth has fashioned belief in the way Chéri de Mendoza sees the Ute Chief as part of his own imaginary panoply, and his own sense of racial solidarity, of markets and colonies. Listening quietly, the Chief silently bemoans the erosion of all belief and all sense of value, while nonetheless casually prolonging the enslavement of his wife and all women in his society. In Otto Warning's magnificent account of his childhood memory of Mormon society, what is the warning offered? Can he do more than stand and stare? And what of his own special deafness as voices from everywhere cascade into his story – is he simply overwhelmed and still unaware? First as a reader and then a translator, I was watching, and over a period of years progressively overwhelmed by Apollinaire's astonishingly varied ways of illuminating the imprisonments of the mind.

You remember the demagogic frenzy of wild and empty belief that's induced in Salt Lake City, and its fantastic effects as Otto describes them on both mind and body. Crowd fanaticism has its own rhythms, and once again rhythm carries the text forwards. Once again I felt I was translating as much with my ears as my dictionaries and thesauruses, along with all the little online digressions that formed a now silenced accompaniment to *Seated Woman*. Without rhythm there is no tone, and without tone there is no context. The tone and pace of each of the narratives in the novel, each from a different time, all needed to be audible again for the text as a whole to speak to an English-language moment now, equally riven by disease, despair, false hope, manipulation, segregation, public narcissism, and rampant fabulation. I've been trying in this essay to say something about how rhythm in language sounds to me, and how I've tried to fashion it to the tunes of Apollinaire's relentless cultural, affective and ethical questioning. But I find I've done little more than digress. Perhaps it couldn't have been otherwise, for me at least. In this journey rhythm has been a matter of words with the right amount of syllables as well as the right meaning; of sentences that respond in their own way to the length of Apollinaire's ones and especially their syntax. And it's been a matter of departing from Apollinaire's rough and ready tone so as to maintain it, and from his polished one so as to nurture it.

In a conversation I had with Margaret Jull Costa I asked her what advice she might have for anyone starting out on a literary translator's journey, and her enormously encouraging reply was read, read, read. My reading in innumerable silent ways has informed my own sense of rhythm and the word-sound world where I try to evoke the rhythm of others. For how different all the story-telling voices sound in *La Femme assise*, not only from each other but from people speaking French and English now. My hope is that this sound-scape, developed over the time that absorbs me and in which I disappear, will form the basis of an open and loose relation between Apollinaire, his translator, his translator's reader, and his extended investigation of war, chaos and despair, and yet still energy, and still faith in society.

XII

Shadow-boxing with the fabulation and fantasy I felt myself in an intimate partnership with Michel Décaudin, the editor among many other volumes of the complete prose works of Guillaume Apollinaire. From Décaudin's work it's clear that to show their effects, Apollinaire needed aspirations and fantasies of dominance, resentment, creativity and diversity all to be rooted in documented reality. This reality has the outlines of a shape that dissolves in the moment, and ranges from specific ways of talking and gesturing, to Mormon dogma, practice and architecture, and to the Medieval Nine Worthies plucked from legend to symbolise chivalry and a life of idealisation and death. There is also the reality shaped by the memoir, a kind of life-writing that Apollinaire allows to percolate layer upon filter upon layer. Think of the astounded the fictional encounter of Brother John Taylor and Victor Hugo at the barricade, which invented though it is recalls Hugo's own memoir of the 1852 barricades, *Histoire d'un crime*, not published until 1877 with Napoleon III long since ousted. First-hand experience, attribution, unconscious projection – who can disentangle them, with each one of us as besotted as the next by our own world view, especially those besotted by power? It's as though to investigate the embroilments of fantasy and society, Apollinaire needed authentic detail and fake authenticity to coincide.

To produce that effect in English I needed to re-dramatise it, to incorporate Décaudin's work in my writing, which means bear witness to it in silence. Perhaps fantasies them-selves work by covering their own historic and psychological tracks, and perhaps sometimes translation does so as well. Fantasies take form and effect whatever we do, perhaps, and all the creativity in the world is needed to show how they shape us and how we shape them.

Three appearances of the seated woman punctuate the score of *La Femmes assise*. The first is the allusion in the title to the painting with almost the same title by Picasso, *Femme assise, Seated Woman*, which now gives its title to my English translation of the novel. The painting is a floating absence in Apollinaire's book, which in its original state has the plain cover of La Nouvelle Revue Française, its publisher. But in the book you're reading now, the painting is shown in plain sight on the cover, an opening visual observation like the visual punctuation marks I've introduced into the novel and this essay too. I wanted them all to act as pointers to some of the allusions and echoes that resonate as Apollinaire shapes this narrative, and rather than pin them own I wanted let them reverberate again, however differently.

Femme assise, then – and the optimism of the Cubist belief I mentioned before, by which the human body can be fragmented in art, and inclusive rather than tyrannical points of view can be found, or if not, invented. But even though colour was thought to distract from that plan, and thought to make painting decorative rather than transformative, the dark colouring of this portrait is itself affecting, it anticipates the war on human bodies and the destruction of society to which the novel bears such bleak witness – bleak, grotesque, satirical, hilarious, vicious, witty, loving, perplexed, melancholic, speculative, moral, humble, patient, ambitious, and filled with life.

She appears again in Otto Warning's account of Mormon society in Salt Lake City. A vast papier mâché model of a seated woman advances slowly in the parade, the enormous parade with all the colours an all the sounds and all the peoples of the world. It's high point in the novel, where moments of high-octane intensity disappear on the wind of association and impulse. She's on a float on wheels with men inside pedalling away furiously, loudly incanting the myths of their own making, their fantasies of gigantic power alluring enough to entice, and false enough to control.

And finally there she is again at the end of the novel. It began with Elvira Swig and at the end, she's left to ponder. By now she's practising the Mormonism in reverse she's been musing about all along, it has no pretention to matriarchy, it's a repetition in miniature, and reverse, of the carnivalesque, patriarchal perversity that has its hooks into Salt Lake City. But the much smaller scale and the reversed gender organisation has other repercussions, even if still emerging through the profusion of male narrative viewpoints in the story. By now Elvira is making her own way in the art world with the work of her own eye and her own hand. Leaving aside the use-value to her four lovers' affections, she doesn't exploit the labour of others and her own labour is hers alone. She assiduously paints images that people want to see and to buy, while still true to painting the world as she sees it. Nicolas, the longest-standing of the four lovers, and perhaps the most prevaricating and the weakest, admires her fakery, by which he means emotional fakery and infidelity. But his benign and inactive criticism, centred on male angst and nostalgia, still opens up the text to a nameless, far more generalised voice, probably still a male one, but perhaps one that floats far enough above to allow people to wonder.

He compares her to the Swiss five-franc coin known as *la femme assise* in French and *Seated Helvetica* in English. *Seated Woman*. A well-known coin at the time, not just in Switzerland but across Europe and especially in Paris; and especially the fake one constantly in circulation. And there she is, the seated woman on the 'tails' side of the coin. She's reaching out as though to her people and as national icons will, and just like the Elvira she seems to point a brush at a painting still to be seen. Icon and imaginary painter reach past their filters into the blue yonder.

And someone whispers in our ear how the need for a better life is made a mockery of in the endless flow of consumerism; but that fakery involves artifice and artifice has the power to transform; and that whether in quaint-fake female colours or not, with imagination the despair of the phallic can be undermined, and its murderous me-and-not-you self-regard; that an interaction between a text, its translation and its reader might re-kindle the desire for open society; and that artifice, insecurity, and the loosening of fixation might finally erode the killing fields of fear, and the fantasies of righteousness and absolute power.

Je donne à mon espoir tout l'avenir qui tremble comme une petite lueur au fond de la forêt

To my hope I give the whole future which trembles like a glimmer deep in the forest

Guillaume Apollinaire

Intermezzo 1

Perhaps you love music, any music. Or perhaps you prefer the movies, or immersion in reading, anything from fantasy to philosophy, or sports live or on the screen, or wandering about in any number of museums of the image. What is it you're enjoying, that's sent you there and keeps you there until the next thing? If someone is playing a concerto with a band and you're moved, or someone else is performing a song, preforming with their voice all the voices in a song, or a dancer is miming with their body allusions to your soul, what are you hearing and seeing? Or how are you hearing? Looking for the composer or looking at the performer? Looking at the performer to find the composer? Looking for anyone to answer the question, why is this so moving? Or energizing. Or infuriating. In any case a network of allusions to an answer and a person or a voice or a body constructed so as to reply. Or illuminate. Or validate. Or pour love. But there's nothing constructed at all. Nor is that what you're looking for either. Allusion upon mnemonic upon projection, all sketching ephemeral understandings of how you've been living, what you've been seeing and of what you hope to see. Everything passes, everything accumulates, everything is consumed, built and superseded.

A translation is never a pane of glass, something to look straight through at whatever you're trying to see beyond; nor something just as easily to shatter when it offends. It'll always be a reading because it always has readers, also commentators and gatekeepers, with whom as individual readers we sometimes identify. We may project our desires and anxieties, and what we hear of their voices comes to weave what we hear of our own, as we wander about anxiously trying to find what it is we're hearing, whether we'll ever get to the bottom of it and find the true word. But perhaps a true word speaks only to deceive, and the glass is illuminated in the many colours of darkness. As a point of view emerges at intersections with so many others, visibility and invisibility take the same dazzling forms.

In translating *Seated Woman* I was aware both of swimming in the sounds of Apollinaire's voice, and in my own way of hearing them. There was nothing else, I suppose, but equally, there was little chance of disentangling openness to a text from appropriating it and closing it off. Little chance or none, other than in the practice of offering words, sentences, tonalities and rhythms: like Apollinaire's I wanted never them to pause, but instead lead on to further wonder – all the digressions and episodes of this miniature epic, that speaks to so many moments of public and private warfare, and invention as well as despair. If words never quite say what they mean, my own self-consciousness as a translator could only hope to match for flimsiness and volatility the one in the writing I was immersed in, and which I love. In the end Elvira Swig plays the markets of art and desire, and abandoning the lures of heroism and violence, invents her own manner of survival, creativity and independence in whatever measure the material pressures on her allow. She's one character in a tapestry of many, each so loosely interwoven with the others that barely a shape emerges. And so now the drama of self-awareness no sooner affirmed than eroded continues in the negotiations of text and translation and the veils of their embrace.

So rather than trying over and over to measure the distance between text and translation text, what if instead I gave free rein to its mobility, and allowed distance between one text and the other to interact with proximity of the two, and create different spaces for reading altogether – for reading the two together? The range of emphasis involved in the interplay of reading, responding and translating is then indefinite, I found. And I wondered whether it might free readers still further, and also me as a practitioner, from trying the find the imaginary vanishing point where a text and its translation fit like a hand in a glove. At least for a moment, during which people might find a renewed contact with what they're seeking in reading, and reading a translation. What does it mean? But still more, how does it mean, how does it mean to us, as individual readers in an imaginary community of readers? A fragmented one as well, and all the better for it.

In what's come before the emphasis was on rendering, writing, and re-discovering in English Apollinaire's short novel. What follows is another sort of response, this time to short narratives by Apollinaire, where the translator's voice is differently integrated in the voice of the person responding. Or integrated differently. As I said earlier, Walter Benjamin turns to Apollinaire's *Le Poète Assassiné*, *The Assassinated Poet*, to say something of how artists, in times of cold and bloody geopolitical destruction, turn to the imagination for a last crusade. It seemed to me that in my own imagination, the proximity of the voices in me of reader-writer-responder-translator could be further witnessed; and that taking them together, another light beyond my own imagining might be cast on the meeting places of radical art and populist disregard for humanity.

Back down to earth, or the page, I'm leaving it to you, the reader, to pick up my small indications of the seams between one voice and the other, one way of writing and another, one or other way of working, writing and translating. The alternation is once again a matter of rhythm – how else to judge when translating what I was hearing would say more than writing about it or describing it?

Apollinaire began in 1913 thinking about collecting together the short narratives that would become *Le Poète assassiné*, before the start of the war and in the same year as *Alcools* was published, as well as *Les Peintres cubistes, méditations esthétiques*. He completed the book in 1914 before enlisting, it was published in 1916, prescient in relation to the War rather than a response to its reality. It displays the historical violence done to voices of creativity, invention and dissent, and beyond even all that it anticipates *Seated Woman* in the way a multiplicity of voices in the head, not only in literature but life, combine invention, confusion and despair. That confusion of what's heard in what fails to be heard not starts again in the process of translation, and is testified to in the shifting pendulum of creativity and receptivity that occupied me in the following pages. They are a response to the first and last narrative in the sequence called 'Le Poète assassiné' and which gives the book its name.

Invention and Disaster

Le Poète assassiné

Poised. Suspended. Hanging alone, and together. Balanced, but unhinged. A touch that hovers over phantoms and debauched guffaws. The freedom of wit caught up in the rules of spontaneity. The generosity of play, but also its violence. Apollinaire's fiction is barely fiction at all, reading it feels like getting dressed, moving into the clothes of life and wearing them, but also watching them, in those silent observations which seem to need art to survive. Thought and its disarray. Ambition and its wanton scattering. Humour and disaster.

Ease of access then, snug as a bug, knife through butter? There are certainly many amusing anecdotes and turns, and hilarity is everywhere. But smiles and giggles can be slow-burning as well, they creep up, they develop over the time, especially the time of different readings, and echoes begin to fester and irritate the memory. Opening books on Apollinaire, anyone is faced with a choice: books that show scholarship spilling everywhere, scholarship of Apollinaire's own scholarship going off in all directions, mythological, historical, cultural, also the whimsical and the impulsive, and drifting off in auto-biographical fits and starts; or on the other hand, books that hide it. It is like choosing between showing or hiding the tracked changes in a Word document, seeing or not seeing the paths to a finished piece. It is a vast commonplace that the digital has transformed not only the opportunities of scholarship but the ways of using it and enjoying it. Commonplace itself fascinates Apollinaire, and this one resonates with his own never-ending, at once enthusing and melancholic, labyrinthine fascination with the modern, his own modern-day ways of engaging with the world. Bolts from around the blue world turn benign as we come to understand them, they might even become friends, or anyway familiar props in the meeting places where what we know turns into what we wear. Creative or alienating? Does progress signal greater understanding of the present or simply greater ignorance of the past? The modern look expresses our own way of seeing and using the world, it is the idiom of our day, of life lived with no fear of loss. But gaiety and spontaneous consumption also signal a passive enjoyment of the here and now, and the loss of anything else. Tracking down Apollinaire's frequently obscure allusions using internet resources is a very different experience from reading about them in notes to learned editions of his writings. Each has its own story to tell, one of immediate access and reverberation, the other of the work, life and generosity of the editors, and both tell a story of Apollinaire himself, his absorption in learning for its own sake, its store-houses of surprise and its prison-houses of orthodoxy.

There are any number of ways of imagining Apollinaire following his private leads, his silent enthrallments in the Bibliothèque nationale, rue de Richelieu, or the Bibliothèque de l'Arsenal, two of his favourite haunts. *Le Poète assassiné*, *The Assassinated Poet*, is a frightening title which speaks of the violence done to the right to think and speak. What it does not show immediately, and what insinuates itself into the imaginings of the reader, undermining my patience but soliciting my fragile sense of purpose, is the censorship, fear, deafness and resentment woven into education, scholarship and learning, into the silent voices of learning as well as the loud ones, and along routes as unpredictable as ways of thinking and remembering are themselves endless. Facility with styles will not get to the bottom of these highways and byways, and Apollinaire's deftness with the written voice flirts with horror as well as ecstasy, or just suspicion and fun. But urgency seeps through everything, even the flippant, an urgent desire to be on the move and not miss anything, to be there and a witness. Creating and simple recording seem to rely on each other, highlighting moments when anything creative is overwhelmed, and still packed with an energy of their own.

* * * * * *

A sexually irreverent approach to kinship and work characterizes the birth of our poet whose assassination is foretold. The image of his illegitimacy bounces off at a point into a chorus of midwives singing in a harmony only possible on the page: each to her own, her own body, enclosure and whim. The lyrical reaches out to the communal and stops. Then there is death in childbirth, the travelling optimism of the father and widower turned gambler, his staged suicide when all is lost, his money as well as any hope of hooking up with anyone. Now we find the poet-to-be orphaned and under the tutelage of another traveller, witness to these rapid and barely noticeable events, a Dutchman with a taste for Humanist and Enlightenment thinking. The natural world and the social one are both organized by love – so imagines this tutor wishing happiness for his pupil, and generally seeking love as much as reason with a distant Rousseau-esque air. Uncertainty and faintness turn into an improvisation on the who and the where; and on the name. The collapse of love, but also the love of life both grow in the nomadic existence of the poet-thinker-vagabond, the Dutchman believes; but in its unpredictability, light or dark, the poet's life is both unique and common to everyone, like life at large, and loss. For the Dutchman the mobility of souls is a life force, he draws on the Ancient theory of metempsychosis and extends it to objects, souls pass not just from one body to another in endless life, but from the animate to the inanimate. Life is breathed everywhere, not only in all the living world but, in a moment of spontaneous lyricism, even in the dust of the streets and the roads: the ashes of the living and of life itself?

This is a life of universal community, a re-awakening to the word, always on the move, binding things together and people. The word triggers memory and is itself absorbed in memory's tapestry. Some of the rabbis are turned to as living proof, thought to have the same soul that occupied the bodies of Adam, Moses and David, we are told; and the Hebrew letters aleph, daleth and mem which their names share are invoked as living proof. These letters themselves travel via the alphabets of Phoenician, Aramaic, Arabic, Greek and Latin. Has the meme of metempsychosis survived, or lost out and disintegrated in this alphabetical replification, in which its source is as much lost as re-discovered, and in the same breath? In Apollinaire's eye selfishness is not circumscribed, but empowered and dissipated in genetics and evolution. Culture seems to grow and stagnate in the same breath. Perhaps that's the salvation of the self and the ego, its only route to creativity, but it cannot be chosen, it's as passive as it's practised or willed. This moment of improvisation, episodic and invisibly demarcated, ends there, as vulnerable to disappearance as the anonymity of the Dutchman himself, the widower-nurturer suspended somewhere. If souls reappear in whatever form, perhaps there is nothing new and creation is at a standstill. I wish you happiness as though I were always wishing people happiness, just something to say and the words we use, and as though happiness were forever out of reach and beyond understanding.]

* * * * *

But what sort of wish is it, nonetheless, and what does it say about the longed-for interaction of poetry and education? Asking the question contributes, it seems, to losing the answer. In Apollinaire, as in Flaubert before him and Sebald or Pamuk after, covering the traces of learning is part of learning: learning and forgetting absorb each other. The excitement created by ceremonial plaques expropriated from Benin into the museums of Europe covers over the violence by which they are viewed there on not in West Africa, now forgotten in the moment. Ways have to be found of asking without asking, in other words without presupposing the answer, and it seems that fiction provides that mode of thinking with a vessel. Learning is wrapped up in influence, to learn is in part – but what part? – to be aware of influence, to recognise it, to adopt positions and attitudes in relation to it. But to learn is also to learn that influence cannot be recognised, it's wrapped in the ways it's recognised and lost there. The more an influence is seen the more it hides in plain view. It seeps through the pores of anyone's spontaneity. The translations of influence into ways of knowing cannot simply be made visible by strategic acts, which serve as much to hide as reveal. The vast error which Sartre addresses throughout his writing, culminating in the huge work on Flaubert, of privileging prose over poetry, organization over sensation, is a dramatization of this confusion of influence and voice. Apollinaire explores this unseeing vision in wandering between his own domains of poetry and prose, separate and combined, each hovering all the time between invention and disaster.

Hilarity and illegitimacy have set the stage. Croniamantal, our poet, steeped in thoughts on love and the word, turns his full attention, such as it is, to medieval legend, like many before him. Don Quixote has already merged with La Fontaine in the story of what makes Croniamantal tick, and La Fontaine will emerge again shortly in a loud but unplaced echo. He gets bounced into a contemporary version, and an inept one, of the art of the fable. So: ineptitude, or satire? Both are possible, it depends on you and me as readers, on who we imagine is listening – but to what? Croniamantal has only ears for Arthur's round table and future lovers. In the sweat pushed out by ideas being pushed in, scream the silent screams and aches of sex-need. He wanders by Italian workers repairing the road surface, and the voice of the narrative veers off into the etymology of the words they use. The French 'câlin', meaning affectionate and cuddly, drifts narratively backwards and forwards in time, as well and sideways across frontiers, to evoke a local usage 'calignaire', meaning girl-friend or boy-friend, lover, sweetheart, suitor, betrothed. But science and fantasy rub shoulders. We have only the narrative voice to believe in, which tells us that Croniamantal has learned this usage and at some point has absorbed its provenance, just as readers are drawn into believing what we are told. 'Calignaire' is just a word Croniamantal knows, like he knows the legends of King Arthur, and now I know it too, or think I do. History has turned to legend and returned into it, each is the placenta of the other. Etymology joins forces with fantasy, knowledge with received knowledge, and together they forge the attachments of which orthodoxy is made and which give it life.

Where are we? In the narrative, this is a place dissolving in its own mobility and the mobility of its telling. Croniamantal could be walking anywhere, unless he is riding by like an imaginary knight: perhaps Don Quixote has returned to the scene, but so distantly that the echo is silent and the laughter has gone quiet. Suspended between the languages with which he is familiar, Croniamantal is affected in the moment by Boccaccio's medieval Italian along with the Provençal French of the same period. Nothing unusual there, or in the combination of languages, registers and usages from anywhere making up anyone's idiom. But all the mobility and all the wit in all the associations of hearing and speaking cannot break the loudly inaudible iron web of sex and obedience. 'Calignaire' may be a local word but the locality itself could be anywhere, its uniqueness is not protected. Ironically, the illustration of its meaning given by the online *Trésor informatisé de la langue française* is this very sentence of Apollinaire's. Croniamantal is Croniamantal is Croniamantal, from invention to dictionary and back again; and his own silent cry for sex is not only lost but enclosed in his voice voiced in voices. Nostalgia voices gaping vulnerability.

* * * **

He got back on his horse and took the road to his home. Unhappy in love for the first time, he saw the extremes of melancholy in the countryside he had ridden across earlier. The sun was low on the horizon. The grey leaves of the olive trees were filled with a sadness just like his own. Shadows stretched in a flow around him. The river where he had seen the women bathing was abandoned now, and the quiet noise of the water made unbearable fun of him. He spurred his horse to the gallop, and then it was dusk, and lights began to shine in the distance. When night fell he reined in his horse and drifted into a frantic reverie. The slope had cypress trees on either side, and in the gloom of the night and the gloom of love Croniamantal followed the path to melancholy.

* * * **

In the first days of 1911. Poems scribbled down and kept in a cigar box are the last things just evoked. In narrative, changes of perspective can be made to feel like an eruption of different sensations – not new ones necessarily, or if they are new, they produce a return of associations and thoughts which are still without shape. After all these years. The new and the rediscovered illuminate each other but also absorb each other. Apollinaire's disregard for chronology and for unity of tone is not organised in a premeditated attack on narrative, cultural expectation or ways of knowing. It doesn't sound at all like an anticipation of postmodern self-importance, the affective stakes are too high, and attachments are still the stuff of life, love and grief. Nor does it read like the complexity of Proust, its epistemology is more intuitive and impulsive. Apollinaire's sense of the contingent is temporal: life as it's lived. His melancholy arises from the disappearance of everything in sequence, and his excitement comes from sequence too, the emergence of the new to replace what once was there. If things disappear and are then forgotten, the colours of the new are easily created, too easily, with every appearance of spontaneity and authenticity.

In the first days of 1911. These could be first days lived by anyone, and then the phrase has no meaning to anyone, or else has meaning to anyone and no-one. And yet still, the date... It comes from before our time, and if it reaches out to readers now, it does so by gradually moving up on people, perhaps the effects resume, perhaps they overwhelm, perhaps they dissolve. This date opens a tiny bit of narrative in which Apollinaire gives voice to the avant-garde of the pre-1914 period, in Paris and Berlin particularly, that early twentieth-century Renaissance in all art; this is Apollinaire's way of offering it again to his community of readers just as the start World War 1 was beginning to loom. How do the two relate – a person's own way of engaging with things, and the offerings and intrusions of others? The year 1911 and the tone in which it appears engage with you as a reader on the basis of not knowing you. An everyday feature of reading is turned into the ambition of this avant-garde moment, simply a different moment, not fatally connected with the moment now of reading. Disconnection seems to be needed for invention, the only way for it resist repetition: invention cannot be invented, it seems. In the first days of 1911. Where might I have been in the first days of any year, and where might you? Nostalgia, attachment; detachment, and translation from one point of view to another: all are in this together, in a ballet without contact or touch, but which breathes embrace nonetheless.

In 1909, Marinetti's *Manifeste du futurisme*, *Futurist Manifesto* had already pushed its way onto the front page of *Le Figaro*. Apollinaire had risen to the visual examinations of speed in the pictures of Boccioni and Severini, a speed hoping to shape the ability of all voices to speak together and even at the same time. Solidarity of experience was now making the solidarity of modern meaning, and a force with which to challenge the directed thought and all its divide-and-rule compartmentalizations. Apollinaire is energized by what Clive Scott calls this 'dissolution or multiplication of human identity'. But he also wonders about the speedy switch from living forms, from living with forms and re-making them, to an easy and joyous consumption of them. The fits and starts of the living mind, the clatter and crash of the old and the new and the old again all sound far more potent to him, and far more threatening as well it seems. And by 1914 as he was putting *The Assassinated Poet* together, 1911 might have appeared bathed in its own purity, the simple capacity floating everywhere to ask the question still in such need of an answer: in the name of what power is power fragmented and re-formed?

Toneless explosiveness. Pieces of description chaotically assembled. The great cries and the distant angers of the city. But there is still the sensation of continuity in reading his narrative, taking us far back and inward, the familiarity of that sense of inwardness returns, it spreads a clarity over all the shifts of content and tone and the sharp intakes of breath. Joy and anxiety together conjugate anticipation. Eyelids turn into jaws and devour the world, both seen and unseen. Vision is taken out from inside the eye, away from physiology altogether, and is put onto the surface of the body outside. It's re-discovered and re-shaped *on* the body, in combinations both monstrous and empowering. There's nothing sensuous about this figure with jaws for eyelids. Nor alarming either, in the end. Instead this whole little piece is made up of propositions rather than equivalences, and their basis is under construction; and so it also dissolves. Will individual sensations of life form the basis of renewed understanding, or not? Can readers even be sure what of the sensations being evoked, or of what they mean?

Sensations nonetheless indicate the kind of relation that's being forged, they open up the possibility of reaching beyond the already known. My sense of the familiar is not the same as yours, even if it neighbours it.

Understanding needs to be suspended to be renewed; but how can it then be communicated if not sensually, swimming in the endless mediations of life? 'Il mit l'éternité en miettes', he put eternity to the sword, he devoured endless time with his jaw-eyes, he ground away the lines of vision which enclose each one of us. Each one of us faces division and enclosure in this unresolved play of suspension and continuity. But each reader is offered an invitation to explore inwardly the dissolution of our sense of self. And being moved combines optimism with anonymity.

In the first days of 1911, a badly dressed young man was running up the hill of rue Hudon in Montmartre. He had an exceptionally mobile face which expressed the connections between the extremes of joy and anxiety are connected – or so it seemed. Croniamantal followed him to a door with a note on it saying 'Studios This Way'. Autobiography combines with a moment in cultural history. But why? What is the story Apollinaire is telling, and the one given anyone individually to hear? What can be learnt from these disguises, not simply by trying to say what they mean, but trying to follow the way the voices are bound up in each other and live? The combination of personal anecdote, contingency, narrative adventure and fantasy is clear, I think; but that thought involves imagining that this is clear to everyone differently. The there and not there of this blended melancholy, also of this optimism untroubled by origins and traces, resonates differently in each one of us. The sudden flattening of time when speaking uncluttered to a loved one lost in clutter; or showered in the light and the lightness brought in by a lover; speaking together as though skin had dimensions all its own. The joy of waiting and the fear of never understanding.

The books piled on the shelves looked like pats of butter. And as it pushed at the draughty door, the wind brought in unknown beings lamenting all known pain in their tiny cries. All the she-wolves of distress would then screech behind the door, ready to devour the herd, the shepherd and his friend, and prepare there and then the foundation of the new City. Inside the studio there were joys in all colours. There was a window along the whole north wall, with only the blue sky, like a woman singing. Croniamantal took off his overcoat which fell to the ground like a body fished from the sea, sat on the sofa and looked for a long time without a word at the painting standing on the easel. Dressed in blue canvas and barefoot, the painter looked at the picture as well, where two women in the freezing mist were remembering.

To be close to this way of painting and is neither to show nor describe it. It is more like finding a painting by allowing it to melt into others.

Remembering it needs its own way of... remembering: of imagining the possibilities of remembering it, reading and re-reading it, hearing the inward voices which form anyone's relation to things and to others. Picasso's women, those that Apollinaire had seen, and seen transform, combine freedom from the imposed and visible shapes of the body with the shapes the body assumes in pain, or freedom: the body imagined in pain, or freedom. The picture on the easel is not there as we read the page, it lives in reading, formed, unformed and de-formed, formed again by the disconnections of word and image. The cries of pain, timeless, pointless, or on the other hand the pain of birth and re-conception – all pain is lamented; or contemplated: in any case projected on a surface which is there only in these words. The narrative both combines word and image and detaches them from each other. And in juxtaposition rather than harmony,the tiny voices of singular pain sing with myth in the wind. Myth has turned into the legendary, then the familiar, over time, but without understanding, leaving the new city simply to emerge and in that way to be founded at last. Is it the city of freedom or empire? In combining ever differently, does the diversity of colours sing in a new voice or confirm the old? What should we think of the newness in which things appear, does it seduce us into thinking or just seduce? The City of God waits to become the city of each one of us individually, waits to be born now, in reason and respect. The joy of the blue sky is framed for each one of us as we watch, and imagine poet and painter watching together, each to his own. Everything remains to be done.

In this studio leaking breath, vision and voice, joy is connected to melancholy and fear, is disconnected from them too. The clarity of joy and the clarity of fear is the clarity in which each is disguised in the other. The blue of Picasso's blue style, which infiltrates some of the ones to follow, challenging period, moment and place, is simply worn on his clothes. In a further flattening effect, which is the opposite of monotonous, these clothes are made of canvas, which is the conventional surface material of painting. Active and passive are re-fashioned, each melts in the other in the forms of individual taste and everyday impulse. The painter is making the work and the poet is discovering it, and they contemplate together without yet knowing what is being made, or in what collaboration. They watch still women remembering, they watch the frozen fascination of remembering itself, the echoes of a past belonging only to each one, and to you. But a different memory is born just the same: born as much as hidden in the clear light, and in the company of readers together, alone.

The blue of the bright sky framed for you extends the memory of blue in Picasso's pictures. But here we find work is lost in life, blue is the colour of the painter's clothes. Anyone could find themselves imagining this blue on the loose, the colour of any moment of surprise by joy or catastrophe. It is transported back onto a picture living in the unique sound of these words, which reaches out to the distant sounds of memory being reformed. Blue and its stylization continue their travels inwards and outwards, propelled by melancholy towards optimistic living.

* * * * *

There was also something implacable in the studio, a big piece of broken mirror was hung on the wall with hooks. It was a bottomless, vertical dead sea at the bottom of which there was an untrue life breathing life into nothing. Opposite art there is the appearance of art, of which people are unafraid and unaware, and which demeans them just when art uplifts them. Croniamantal hunched over further and further with his arms on his knees, he looked away from the painting and his eyes rested on a card on the floor with these words written on it in paint:

> Gone to the bar.
> The Bird of the Benign

Imagine the new quivering in style; imagine watching it grow in flights of the benign and the generous. Fantasy flights, perhaps. From Benin to Paris in any case. The distances are so varied and indeterminate that they become in themselves a witness to life. And after all, Croniamantal's life as a poet has already begun, and so has his author's. Where it begins and where it is found are questions unanswered and lived. This generative – or is it? – confusion of beginnings itself begins in a hilarious jumble of satire and lyricism, mythology and medicine: doggerel and melody too.

Prospectus for a New Remedy.

> Elle prit le soleil
> Et le plongea dans la mer

Ainsi les ménagères
Font tremper un jambon dans la saumure
Mais malheur! Les saumons voraces
On dévoré le soleil noyé
Et se sont fait des perruques
Avec les rayons
Maï Maï ramaho nia nia

A daughter of Donegal sings to the distant sound of Celtic songs sending heroes on their way. But legendary language is losing its depth and memory speaks in the echoes of our time, the momentary activities of the day. But perhaps what appears as day to day flatness has new stories to tell instead of the old ones of depth and distant swan songs. The sea into which stars fall and from which they rise again is simply brine as well as the stuff of mythology – brine for preserving, and also good for a stock. But there are salmon in this brine, and unlike the ham being soaked they are still alive, and meat-eaters all of a sudden, and they simply polish it off. Despite pulling in opposite directions, brine and salmon sing a little assonantal song together, the confusion of category does not appear alienating, and this glow of the now, of present living, is made out of a hilarious irreverence for the past and anything symbolic. The vastly different Apollonian and Romantic ways of adoring the sun going up or down are divested both of rational power and inward depth – in fact of any depth of association at all. Instead sun adoration is translated sideways into an interest in wigs; and produces a concentrated and surreal little satire of fashion and all the guises of seeing.

But what about the chorus which returns at the end of each stanza? It reads like a phonetic evocation in French of a song without words, or just humming. Or like a sound-sketch of a French sound-idea of singing; French ideas of the Celtic and the folkloric. Things still remain unplaced, because they are experienced affectively, from the inside: these are subjective sounds as well as generally French ones. The self is spilling over into the non-self, but still does so in its own way. The stories of travel away and into the past of others are translated into French simply by being understood in a French ear. On the other hand, the inventiveness of the French sound-sketch surprises me as anyone into recognizing sensations and memories I had thought unique to me, and without voice. Everywhere hilarity exceeds limits which are then re-formed in the chorus, where for a moment melancholy adds its own notes to this little community of song.

But it is soon lost in the rest, Croniamantal's first foray into modernist irregular verse goes off in any number of directions: after all the whole point of free verse is to adapt. On the other hand, Croniamantal's starting effort is wrapped in obscurity, and understanding something easily slips into not understanding at all. A sense of false knowledge burgeons and drifts away in these random as well as organized sound patterns, which for that reason also encourage a fascination with etymological sources. The true is fashioned in the false, and guidance dissolves in any number of little labyrinths. Mythology, folklore, etymology, prosody, horticulture, cookery all join in a witty, discordant and energizing harmony which is also pointless. The new free verse multiplies layers and perspectives which may free people from the weight of the past and past thinking, but which bury people just as much under an avalanche of association turned shapeless information. The power of myth to indoctrinate is re- kindled as much as cut loose, and alienation resurfaces in abandoning a place in which to think about how each one of us remembers and forgets.

On the one hand eclecticism, boundless renovation: modernity. On the other consumption, tending to thoughtlessness: modernity. Confusion re-calibrates its own source, the context and the possibilities of life, but at the cost of purpose and a sense of self. But perhaps a sense of identity gets in the way of allowing identity to develop, in any case. On the other hand again, perhaps subjective response does not simply incarcerate people in their own point of view, but does after all generate ways of re-engaging with it. Cubism displays an enjoyment of flatness, displayed also in Brecht's theatre as well as post-modern fiction. In Brecht in particular suspicion of depth creates the basis for a resistance to supposedly impenetrable causes of devastating effects, which can then be presented as outside our control. In Cubism this flat exuberance is also a dark one, visibly without colour, colour is a source of suspicion, attached as it is to the appeal of the way things are and its power, closing our eyes to the *why*. These pictures do not simply abandon perspective, and it is not just a question of multiplying lines of perspective and ways of seeing. There is always another way to look at any picture and its relation to the world beyond, but there is no way of guaranteeing the plurality of seeing. Like remembering, seeing is locked into the moment, which joins with others to make the time of each one of us.

Fragmenting the place and time of seeing also disperses it, now it's everywhere and nowhere, being and not being here combine, and everywhere optimism and melancholy bleeds into each other. Such is

Croniamantal's viewing as he discovers the studio of Benign the Bird for the first time. Even the irreverent extravaganzas of collage express a kind of nostalgia, as though their ambition were beyond reach, the ambition to fragment the frame of vision. Frames emerge from frames as much as from their collapse – frames without end, both visible and invisible. Once out of context and stuck in a new one, any bit of coloured paper, any bit of a letter or a word, any perceptual flotsam spreads liquidly in all sorts of shapes over the surface of the mind. Flotsam and jetsam re-connect with primeval attachments spreading over the indefinite surface tensions of the now, and assuming their form.

* * * **

Love follows the theatre which forges love. Croniamantal is trying to get his play performed, followed by a chapter called 'Love'. The chapter on theatre takes the form of a play, or really an allusion to a script. Tiny little verbal vignettes succeed each other, spoken by... Allusion and invention rub shoulders, the closer they get to each other the flimsier the likelihood of discovering anything new. But at least the flimsy is not the solid, and on that flimsy basis some kind of resistance to vested interest can be imagined, perhaps. But is caricature transforming or confirming what readers already know? Apollinaire seems to be starting again. Passing, somehow pre- categorized anecdotes seem to confirm and not re-direct our ways of knowing and recognising, which is the pleasure we find in them. At the same time, knowing is renewed in lived moments and explodes on their nerve ends. But for how long?

The charm of Apollinaire's transitions, in narrative as well as verse, is in the transition itself: it follows the confusion of remembering and forgetting. In this one love continues in the style of a script, it is prefaced by what sounds like a stage description in spite of the past tense, which makes it sound like story-telling and which displaces and disperses the whole scene. The stage is set, but where is it?

Description, storytelling, and prose monologue all digging inwards and sexualizing everything – verse song erupts in the middle of it all, and spreads the confusion of the new and the desired, with all its imprints of the past. Nursery rhyme idiom is invoked and plugs immediately into the intimate sounds within each one of us, the child lost and living in the adult. But by staying in tune with that model, Apollinaire has invented those sounds and verse-sounds, and they are now untranslatable – that was always their nature. Still, intimacy can be re-made and re-heard at any time, and here the intimacy of everyone is anonymised, atomised, re-inhaled.

But the intimacy of voice does not affect people in the same way. This un-placed, self-dissolving poetry in the making could not be further removed from a political idiom. Equally, a political idiom could not be more easily discovered there. In aching to embrace and smother someone in kisses Croniamantal is steeped in the stories that have marked him. Arthurian legend and Celtic myth are his special favourites. The round moon, round loaves, round breasts, the round table and the round clearing are all confused in the mental forest in which Croniamantal is wandering about like a Prince seeking his Sleeping Beauty. Apollinaire has him start to probe. Not all roundness is the same. These ones are spatial, astronomical, sexual, digestive, mythological, and their confusion once again creates a confusion of depth and flatness. Such is the point of view: at once plural and impregnable. Not even the round table can break it, or make all points of view equal, or equally accessible to one another. The democracy of the round table is a testament to its own failure.

You haven't understood the joke about this clearing at all. Do you really think it's been made round like a round table for the good of man's equality and the equality of the weeks? Days are not alike, you know that. The decent knights sitting at the round table are not equal, one has the sun in his eyes and is blinded by it, then the next one has the sun in his eyes and is blinded by it, and the others have their shadows in front of them. They are all decent and you are decent too, they are no more equal than day and night.

Amorous longing spills over into thoughts on social and communal understanding, the divisions of which it cannot breach and which confirm its own. But still they are not the same. The person who loves me will not love my way of knowing but more my way of being ignorant and unaware. The one who sings and attracts me will be ignorant just as I am and dance a ballet of many fatigues. Sexual need, like any pleasure or pain, is referred to in indefinite and cumulative approximations, and in a mutual non-understanding which might perhaps form the basis of respect. But Croniamantal's quest for any understanding seems unlikely to be completed, or his quest for a community of friends with whom to discover the fantasies they share, sung in the voices known only to each one.

It seems that there is a transparent film of disintegrated myth which attracts people to each other just as much as skin and sweat and saliva; these paths may ever meet, even if they merge, like oil and vinegar or the yoke and white of an egg. Bare arms have become a leitmotif and they make a ballet out of the comings and goings of love and its memories. *S* tay with me my lips are exploding with kisses. Here they come, here they are, they are falling on your head and your hair. I bite your hair and the perfumes of ancient times. I bite your hair which winds like poetry on the pores of a corpse. Death and more death with worms growing like hair. There are kisses on my lips, here they come, here they are on your neck, on your eyes, on your eyes, on your eyes. My lips are exploding with kisses, here they come, here they are, they burn like a fever, they press on you and enchant you, kisses and kisses of panic on your ear, your temple, your cheek. Feel my embraces, bend to the pressure of my arm, be weary, be drained, be weary. There are kisses on my lips, here they come, here they are, kisses and panic on your neck, on your hair, on your head, on your eyes, on your mouth. I ache for the love of you this spring day when the blossoms have gone from the boughs and wait for their fruit to grow.

Go away, go away and far from the perfumes of ancient times in my hair, for you belong to me.

And Croniamantal went away without turning his head and for a long time he could still be seen through the branches, and after he had disappeared his voice could still be heard ever more dimly.
I am a traveller without a stick, a pilgrim without a staff and a poet without a writing case, I am the least powerful of all men, I have nothing left and I know nothing.

And his voice no longer reached Tristouse Ballerinette who was gazing at herself in the stream.

The perfumes of antiquity are spreading over the tips and tangles of affect, of love and longing, just under the skin. Neither myth nor sensation explains the other, the sense of antiquity is not explaining the sensations of affect, even though each confirms the other. Such is authentic time, the lived time of the self and the sense of others; and such are the revelations of history continuously promised by this sense of lived but un-narrated time. The sad-eyed ballerina dances to the rhythm of her time which nobody can hear, for it is their own. From a distance I see her immobile and silent dance, and even as she looks at herself she expresses my own longing. The sad-eyed mechanical ballerina dances to her own time, as it is made and as it makes her, and as it makes me as I watch with longing.

At another level again, in both harmony and unison with the others, Apollinaire himself looks back at looking with longing at his lover, the painter Marie Laurencin, with whom he had parted before the war. Each watches with his own eyes, with her own eyes, and Sad-Eyes hears people loving her with their own hands and eyes. She advises travel, and finding other words and other learning, other hands and verses and kisses with which to touch and squeeze. But all the while she watches her own image refracting and dissolving in the moving waters of her time. People feel in what they know the depths of their limitations stretching over the time of their living. The same feelings are suppressed and also live in silent denial. The mechanism of our knowing performs what we know and what we do not. Now I know nothing and my loving is all one. The image of our knowing is reproduced not just in what we know but the inability to reach it, and there lies its melancholic aura, its loneliness and solidarity combined. Even in continuing to look the other way, in continuing to look as we look, a generous community of people could still be imagined of people looking at what is hidden in their own plain sight.

Croniamantal's sense of being ignorant of everything, of having nothing to learn from or to offer either readers or lovers, echoes in the negative Apollinaire's narrator in 'Les Fiançailles', a sequence of poems which figures in *Alcools* and was first published in 1908. 'Je ne sais plus rien et j'aime uniquement'. Now I know nothing and my loving is unique. The date evokes an intersection. On the one hand, the inward looking experimentation with free verse, the explorations of impulse and primeval voices that seem to reverberate there. On the other, the invasions of the modern, airplanes and radio waves, coupled with the other cultures piling in, the non- European, African and Oceanic masks and fetishes that flooded Paris in these opening years of the twentieth century. Apollinaire the modern versifier meets Apollinaire supporter of Picasso, thinker on Picasso's art since the blue and pink acrobats, which started their still dancing in 1904; and then witness to the explosive birth of *Les Demoiselles d'Avignon* in 1907, which seemed to break the nets of looking and toss them so much more widely. The betrothal is made from broken pieces, but valued for their capacity to remain unique, to relate to each other without fitting together always in the same way, without always benefiting the visible, the apparent, the known, the consumable, the distributable and the saleable, all the illusions of capture, victory, adaptation – but to what?, adjustment and acquisition, suspicion transparent and dark in equal measure. Uniqueness of this kind may finally fragment the point of view rather than confirm it.

But it is a dangerous game. The opening poem of *Alcools*, the last to be written, in 1912, famously ends on sun slit throat. And in 1916, the capacity of Croniamantal, our poet, to speak in tongues turns into the capacity of tongues to speak as one, in a frenzied diversity now smelted into the hatred of all poets. Apotheosis, transcendence, redemption, even fertility – it all both frees and assassinates. What is openness if not the idea of it, then forever claimed and re-claimed and re-owned. A zone cannot remain indeterminate for long. 'Les jours s'en vont je demeure', Apollinaire sings in the very next poem, time passes and here I am, the loneliness of grief is also the devastation of hearing only the sound of your own voice. Apollinaire knows this and speaks it.

* * * * *

One of the most generous readers of Apollinaire I know is Walter Benjamin, his way of reading is made of generosity, he writes of reading in recognition of the overlay of voices heard, perhaps just imagined, in our own way, by each one of us. He stages diversity of voice in his way of writing: his studied erosion of citing and speaking, speaking and remembering, half remembering, not remembering, being lost in mnemonics – what other impulses are there to utter a thought? To speak is to speak as me and mine, to remember and forget in equal measure, in the moment, neither meets the other, each is lost in the other. Benjamin recognises how we hear voices in smothering them, each one of us, and he finds voice for the pathos of our responsibility for hearing, for losing, each one of us.

He evokes Apollinaire through someone else, through an attribution between friends, each living the promise of a new moment, living also pressure and danger. 'Son âme [...] a les caprices de l'océan', his soul has the capriciousness of an ocean, Apollinaire writes in *La Phalange nouvelle* in 1908 of Henri Hertz, a literary journalist, poet and story writer, and voice of the left. In the Chancellerie des universités de Paris there is a Prize named after Henri Hertz, established by his widow, for a work of history, criticism or fiction which communicates the ethical or civic concerns of its time. Benjamin hears this capacity in Hertz himself, and in turn evokes him quoting Apollinaire and gives his own readers in 1929, and now, Apollinaire's voice in the imagined memory of Hertz. Such is the story of how Hertz might have come to hear words such as these:

Open, graves, you, the dead of the picture galleries, corpses behind screens, in palaces, castles, and monasteries, here stands the fabulous keeper of keys holding a bunch of the keys to all times, who knows where to press the most artful lock and invites you to step into the midst of the world of today, to mingle with the bearers of burdens, the mechanics whom money ennobles, to make yourself at home in their automobiles, which are beautiful as armour from the age of chivalry, to take your places in the international sleeping cars, and to weld yourself to all the people who today are still proud of their privileges. But civilization will give them short shrift.

I'm quoting this exhortation and vision in the translation of Edmund Jephcott and Kingsley Shorter of Benjamin's text, *Surrealism: The Last Snapshot of the European Intelligentsia*. It follows a floating appeal inspired by the voice of André Breton in *Nadja*, in 1928: 'what form do you suppose a life would take that was determined at a decisive moment precisely by the street song last on everyone's lips?' In his sequence of quotations, translations, evocations and adaptations, in his writer's travels between them and in the travels he can only hope for of his writing to readers, some close, some far, Benjamin stages the passage he knows from the political to the historical, as he calls them. In the form of his comment, in a narrative staging the dissolution of place and narrative voice, he gives life to his belief that theories high and low live and die in the sensations of historical time, its cues, the lived time of the moment now, once now, already forgotten.

Apollinaire makes a voice that is both his and not his, his Croniamantal drowns in the complexity and the diversity of its own making. At the same time it seeks the simplicity shared with anyone of having a voice, even as that simplicity turns with an equal simplicity into the equal pathos of not knowing how your own voice is made. Unity of voice and purpose is sought for the generosity it offers, and the solidarity in which it might be made; but it is resisted too for the sense if fosters of the right to suppress and to silence. I have tried here to find an appropriate response, I have again felt the proximity of translation and criticism, of translating words that move me into a language I might know, and make a texture where I might find my way, my way of hearing Apollinaire, and the generosity of his witness. Respond, translate, respond again. Listen.

The case of the masked corporal, in other words the assassinated poet. The title of the last of story Apollinaire includes in *Le Poète assassiné* is made of an interplay of masks and resuscitation. The assassinated poet, and poetry annihilated in the pogroms are resuscitated in the masks of our time, anyone's time: the masks in which the present couches the past and absorbs it, silences it and voices it; the masks of our understanding which we share, each one of us alone, and for which we fumble, together.

'So tell me are you wounded?' said our new Lazarus. 'Gunner, this is a mask,' said the mysterious corporal, 'and it hides everything you would like to know and everything you would like to see, and it blacks out the answers to all your questions since you came back to life, it silences every prophecy, and you can thank it for making it impossible for you ever to know the truth again.'

Before the war, in a different voice Apollinaire had written his 'je ne sais plus rien et j'aime uniquement', I finally know how I love, to suspend the knowledge and the blindness given only to me, and to love. Now in the middle of war, in a silent shrieking and with the loudness of a person just standing there, Apollinaire has translated the symbolic masks of knowledge and ignorance into the lived violence of gas masks and head bandages. He lives not just the appropriation of art by war, and not just innovation colonized by investment empires. He lives the love of art and its capacity to speak destruction as much as fertility; and to voice the resuscitation of the masks in which we live, love and destroy.

Our new Lazarus walks past mobilisation posters on his way to re-enlisting in the armoured corps. There will be no end to violence, and resuscitation may only repeat. Such is survival, it seems, in mind as well as body; and yet loyalty is made here as well. In the story these posters appear in the form of one of Apollinaire's favourite idioms, the ideogram. The word and all its ambition to free the mind by re-organizing the relations of seeing and reading is re-embedded in this moment, where appealing posters combine at a distance with mutilation and blood in the mud. What is our measure of such distances? What is our immersion in them? The jingles, the refrains and the slogans on your lips and the banners in your mind may just as easily re-direct as re-assert the psychic shape in which you live, or any of us. Apollinaire re-imagines a beautiful poster with the outlines of a coffin, and makes a flattened image made of words, 'voici le cercueil où il gisait pourrissant et pâle'. Here is the coffin where he lay rotting and pale. Translation may help us listen to the sounds of this assassinated poet, but they will be the beats in our own veins.

Intermezzo 2

And finally, for my pleasure as much as yours, I hope, a translation of a free verse poem by Apollinaire through which I began to see the freedom of translation. It's a freedom to serve as well as discover. A stage where listening serves offering but is disentangled from owning. And that sense of translation is alive in Apollinaire's poem as well. Frantic consumption of modern urban energy is disintegrating, and inwardness discovers its vulnerability and exile. Still it speaks, by being spoken to from a distance measured in disappearance, attachment and wonder. A torn and frayed uniqueness takes momentary shape, smelting together endless lose ends, the rhythms of nothing and everything, and the lyricism of gifts floating in the wind. Published in 1913, the poem tells a story of the art Apollinaire championed, that overwhelmed him in its urgency, rigour and generosity, and to which he replies with an intimate sense of democracy. Just after Apollinaire's death Picasso makes a picture of everything their art has meant to me, perhaps everything it meant to them, in any case a picture of voices shaped in each other and finding whatever it is we each love enough to let live. In the painting and the poem together and across their silent divides, there is music and the imagination of music, movement and the imagination of movement, each jagged and embraceable, each dispossessed and welcoming.

Un Fantôme de nuées

A Phantom in the Skies

As it was the day before the 14th of July
Around four in the afternoon
I went down to have a look at the street entertainers

They're very rarely seen in Paris these days
Turning cartwheels in the air
When I was a boy you saw many more
They've gone to the provinces now mostly.

I walked along boulevard Saint-Germain
And on a little square between the church and Danton's statue
I came across the saltimbanques

The crowd stood silently by
Resigned to the wait
I found a place in the circle where I could see it all
Magnificent weights
Whole Belgian cities held up with a straight arm
By a worker from Longwy
A black and hollow dumbbell with a congealed river for a shaft
And fingers rolling cigarettes as bitter and delicious as life

Various dirty carpets were spread on the ground
Carpets with creases that'll never come out
And almost completely the colour of dust
Carpets with patches of yellow and green
That linger like a tune that won't go away

Can you see the thin and wild one
The ashes of his fathers came out of his beard
He carried his heritage on his face
And looked like he was dreaming of the future
Absently turning the handle of the organ

Its slow tones sang a marvellous lament
Of gurgles and whines and muted groans

The saltimbanques weren't moving
The oldest wore a singlet in that sort of violet pink
On the cheeks of young girls
Somehow close to death

It hides especially in the creases of their mouths
Or by their nose
It's a pink full of betrayal.

There was a man with the treacherous hue
Of his lungs on his back

His arms were everywhere arms were keeping watch

The second saltimbanque
Was dressed only in his shadow
I looked at him for a long time
I've forgotten his face completely
He's a man without a head

Another looked like a thug
An Apache both villainous and good
With his puffed out trousers and suspenders for his socks
Didn't he look like a pimp getting dressed

The music stopped and the bartering began
A penny at a time the crowd threw a pile on the carpet
It was less than the old man wanted for their turns

But when it was clear there was no more to be had
They started their show just the same
A tiny little saltimbanque came out
Under the organ
Dressed in pulmonary pink
With fur on his wrists and fur on his ankles
He made little cries

Bowed nicely spreading his arms
With his hands open wide

Kneeling with a leg behind him
He saluted the four points of the compass
And when he walked on the ball
His slender body turned into a music so delicate
That no-one in the crowd was unmoved
A little spirit quite without human shape
They all thought
And this music of forms
Destroyed the music
Of the mechanical organ
The man was grinding
With his ancestors on his face

The little saltimbanque turned cartwheels in the air
In such harmony
That the organ stopped playing
The organ-player hid his face in his hands
His fingers like descendants of his destiny
Tiny foetuses were coming out of his beard
More cries from the Amerindians
The angelic music of the trees
Disappearance of the child

The saltimbanques were lifting dumbbells with their straight arms
They juggled with the weights

But each spectator looked inside for the miraculous child
Century oh century of clouds

Signposts to Further Reading

Works by Guillaume Apollinaire or about him

Guillaume Apollinaire, *Œuvres poétiques*, préface par André Billy, texte établi et annoté par Marcel Adéma et Michel Décaudin, Éditions Gallimard (Bibliothèque de la Pléiade), 1965

Œuvres en prose, textes établis, présentés et annotés par Michel Décaudin, Éditions Gallimard (Bibliothèque de la Pléiade), I, 1977

Œuvres en prose complètes, Éditions Gallimard (Bibliothèque de la Pléiade), textes établis, présentés et annotés par Pierre Caizergues et Michel Décaudin, II, 1991; III, 1993

La Femme assise, édition originale, Éditions de la Nouvelle Revue Française, 1920

Alcools, translated by Anne Hyde Greet, with a foreword by Warren Ramsey, University of California Press, 1965

Alcools: Poems, translated by Donald Revell, Wesleyan University Press (Wesleyan Poetry series), 2012

Zone, selected poems, introduction by Peter Read, selected and translated from the French by Ron Padgett, NYRB/Poets, 2015

Selected Poems with parallel French text, selected and translated by Martin Sorrell, Oxford University Press (Oxford World's Classics), 2015

Calligrammes, Poems of Peace and War, translated by Anne Hyde Greet, notes and commentary by S. I. Lockerbie, University of California Press, 2004 paperback (1980)

The Assassinated Poet and other stories, translated by Ron Padgett, Carcanet Press, 1985

The Cubist Painters, translated, with commentary, by Peter Read, University of California Press (Documents of Twentieth-Century Art), 2004

Timothy Mathews, *Reading Apollinaire. Theories of Poetic Language*, Manchester University Press, paperback 1990 (1987)

—— 'Looking and Loving: Harlequins in Apollinaire and Picasso', in Literature, Art and the Pursuit of Decay, Cambridge University Press, 2006 (2000).

——'Guillaume Apollinaire, "Lettre-Océan"', in *Twentieth-Century French Poetry: A Critical Anthology*, edited by Hugues Azérad and Peter Collier, Cambridge University Press, 2010

——*The Modernist Bestiary. Translating the Arts through Guillaume Apollinaire, Raoul Dufy and Graham Sutherland*, edited by Sarah Kay and Timothy Mathews, UCL Press, 2020

Peter Read, *Picasso & Apollinaire. The Persistence of Memory*, University of California Press, 2008

Clive Scott, *Translating Apollinaire*, University of Exeter Press, 2014

Other literary and critical works

Dawn Adès, Michael Richardson, Krzysztof Fijalkowski, *The Surrealism Reader: an Anthology of Ideas*, Tate Publishing, 2015

Futurist Manifestos, edited with an introduction by Umbro Apollonio, Thames & Hudson, 1973

Charles Baudelaire, *The Painter of Modern Life*, translated by P.E. Charvet, Penguin Books (Penguin Great Ideas), many editions

The Flowers of Evil, translated from the French by James N McGowan, with an introduction by Jonathan Culler, Oxford University Press (Oxford World Classics), 2008

Walter Benjamin, *Illuminations*, translated by Harry Zorn, with an introduction by Hannah Arendt, The Bodley Head, many editions

One-Way Street and Other Writings, translated by Edmund Jephcott and Kingsley Shorter, with an Introduction by Susan Sontag, Verso, many editions

Mary Ann Caws, *Pablo Picasso*, Reaktion Books (Critical Lives), 2005

Blaise Cendrars, *Moravagine*, translated by Alan Brown, with an introduction by Paul La Farge, NYRB/Classics, 2004

Complete Poems, translated by Ron Padgett, with an introduction by Jay Bochner, University of California Press, 1992

Timothy Mathews, 'On some antidotes to discontent: Delaunay, Cendrars, Villeglé, in *Time and the Image*, edited by Carolyn Gill, Manchester University Press, 2000

Marjorie Perloff, *The Poetics of Indeterminacy: Rimbaud to Cage*, Northwestern University Press (Avant-garde and Modernism Studies), 1999

Eric Robertson, *Blaise Cendrars, The Invention of Life*, Reaktion Books, 2022

Virginia Spate, *Orphism: The Evolution of Non-figurative Painting in Paris, 1910–14*, Clarendon Press, 1979 (Studies in History of Art and Architecture)

Translations, works on translation and its practice

Currently & Emotion: Translations, edited by Sophie Collins, Prototype, 2016

Lydia Davis, *Essays Two, On Proust, Translation, Foreign Languages, and the City of Arles*, Macmillan, 2021

Qu'est-ce qu'une traduction « relevante »? Carnets de l'Herne, 2008 (1988), translated by Laurence Venuti, *What is a "relevant" translation, Critical Inquiry*, Winter 2001

Harriet Hulme, *Ethics and Aesthetics of Translation. Exploring the Work of Atxaga, Kundera and Semprún*, UCL Press, 2018

Silvia Kadiu, *Reflexive Translation Studies. Translation as Critical Reflection*, UCL Press, 2019

André Lefevere and Susan Bassnett, *Constructing Cultures: Essays on Literary Translation*, Multilingual Matters, 1998

One Poem in Search of a Translator. Re-writing 'Les Fenêtres' by Guillaume Apollinaire, edited by Eugenia Loffredo and Manuela Perteghella, with an introduction by Timothy Mathews, Peter Lang, 2008

José Saramago, *The Cave*, translated from the Portuguese by Margaret Jull Costa, The Harvill Press, 2002

Clive Scott, *Literary Translation and the Rediscovery of Reading*, Cambridge University Press, 2012

W. G. Sebald, *Austerlitz*, translated by Anthea Bell, Random House, 2001

List of Images and Credits

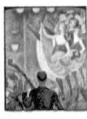

Eugène Carrière, *Portrait du Poète Charles Morice*, 1893
© Clemens Sels Museum Neuss / Walter Klein, Düsseldorf
(photographer)

Jules Pascin, *Hermine au grand chapeau*, 1917
Oil on canvas
Museum of Grenoble.
Image © Jérôme Villafruela, Public domain, via Wikimedia
Commons.

Carl Gustaf Klingstedt, *Tre badande gracer,* no date.
Watercolour on Ivory
Image © CC BY-SA Linn Ahlgren / Nationalmuseum

Luc Albert Moreau, *Seated Woman, Three-Quarter Length*, 1922
Graphite, with stumping and touches of incising on grayish-cream
wove paper, 280 × 210 mm
© 2022. The Art Institute of Chicago / Art Resource, NY/ Scala,
Florence
© Photo SCALA, Florence

Maurice Lourdey, *Edouard de Max dans le rôle d'Homodei dans la
pièce de théâtre de Victor Hugo «Angelo tyran de Padoue»*, 18 February
1905
Le Journal amusant
CC Public Domain

Henri Othon Brauer, *Émile Goudeau, writer,* 1 January 1903
Bibliothèque nationale de France. CC Public Domain

Amadeo Modigliani, *Portrait of Manuel Ortiz de Zárate,*
Pencil on paper, unknown date.
Collection of National Museum of Fine Art, Buenos Aires

Michele Catti, *Portrait of Paul Léautaud*, 1915
CC Public domain, via Wikimedia Commons

Henri de Toulouse-Lautrec, *Aristide Bruant dans son cabaret*, 1893
Lithograph
Metropolitan Museum of Art, New York.
PD CC0 licence

Jorge Manuel Theotocopoulos, *The Martyrdom of Saint Maurice*,
c.1600; oil on canvas, 151.1 × 107 cm.
The Museum of Fine Arts, Houston, The Rienzi Collection, gift of
Mr. and Mrs. Harris Masterson III, 94.885
Photograph © The Museum of Fine Arts, Houston; Thomas R.
DuBrock

February Revolution France 1848. Barricade February 22, 24.
© Chronicle of World History / Alamy Stock Photo

Constantin Guys, *La Grisette*
Coloured ink and watercolour, no date.
CC PD via Wikimedia Commons

Agricol Perdiguier dit Avignonnais la Vertu.
© Aclosund Historic / Alamy Stock Photo

Horace Vernet, *La Bataille d'Isly, 14 August 1844*, 1844–1846
Oil on canvas
Palace of Versailles Collection
CC PD

The Nine Worthies.
Cologne City Hall, Germany
© Raimond Spekking / CC BY-SA 4.0, via Wikimedia Commons

Jacopo Tintoretto, *Last Supper*, 1566
Church of San Trovaso, Venice
CC PD

Umberto Boccioni, *States of Mind I: The Farewells*, 1911 (second series)
Oil on canvas
Museum of Modern Art, New York
© 2022. Digital Image, The Museum of Modern Art, New York/
Scala, Florence. © Photo SCALA, Florence

Robert Delaunay, *Une Fenêtre*, 1912
Musée national d'art moderne, Paris
Public Domain via Wikimedia Commons

Robert Delaunay, *L'équipe de Cardiff*, 1922–23
Musée d'Art Moderne de Paris
CC0 PD licence

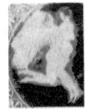

Hyacinthus and the West Wind on a red-figure vase (5th century BCE)
CC PD

Jacques Callot, *Le Combat*, from the series *Le Combat à la barrière*, 1627, Etching
© Princeton University Art Museums collections online
https://artmuseum.princeton.edu/collections/objects/46935.

Ernest Yan' Dargent, illustration for Victor Hugo, *Histoire d'un crime* (1877)
CC PD

Pablo Picasso, *Harlequin*, 1918
© Succession Picasso/DACS, London 2022.